DEATH OF A MINOR POET

As chief of homicide in a major American city, Detective Captain Sam Birge never stops working. So he's not surprised when he gets a call as he's heading home: young man found dead. Birge goes to investigate, and finds young Wesley Gowen dead in an old apartment building. Downstairs is a dingy cafe, upstairs studio apartments, all occupied by artists who insist they know nothing of the murder. When the boy's grieving mother hands over her son's journals, Birge hopes they may contain some clue to the killing, but he suspects they're only filled with the dreams of an unaccomplished poet—who died much too young.

DEATH OF
A MINOR POET

William Krasner

ATLANTIC LARGE PRINT
Chivers Press, Bath, England.
John Curley & Associates Inc.,
South Yarmouth, Mass., USA.

Library of Congress Cataloging in Publication Data

Krasner, William, 1917–
  Death of a minor poet.

  Large print ed.
  1. Large type books.   I. Title.
  [PS3561.R283D4 1985]   813'.54   85–7857
  ISBN 0–89340–874–3 (lg. print)

British Library Cataloguing in Publication Data

Krasner, William
  Death of a minor poet.—Large print ed.—
  (Atlantic large print)
  I. Title
  813'.54[F]   PS3561.R283

  ISBN 0–7451–9083–9

This Large Print edition is published by Chivers Press, England, and
John Curley & Associates, Inc, U.S.A. 1985

Published by arrangement with Atheneum Publishers,
a Division of The Scribner Book Companies, Inc

U.K. Hardback ISBN 0 7451 9083 9
U.S.A. Softback ISBN 0 89340 874 3

Archibald MacLeish quote from 'L'an trentiesme de mon eage,' NEW
AND COLLECTED POEMS by Archibald MacLeish.
Copyright © 1976 Archibald MacLeish.
Reprinted by permission of Houghton Mifflin Company.

T. S. Eliot quote from 'The Love Song of J. Alfred Prufrock,' in
COLLECTED POEMS 1909/1962 by T. S. Eliot, copyright 1936 by
Harcourt Brace Jovanovich, Inc; copyright © 1963, 1964 by T. S. Eliot.
Reprinted by permission of the publisher.

To four boys;
and, with one exception,
their parents.

'Behold, this dreamer cometh. Come now therefore, and let us slay him, and cast him into some pit, and we will say, Some evil beast hath devoured him: and we shall see what will become of his dreams.'

—Gen. 37:19, 20

CHAPTER ONE

Detective Captain Sam Birge thought: The blood's dried by now so it doesn't smell much—just part of the old smells in this dim hall of this rundown apartment building. True, when the body dies the sphincters tend to let go—not all the time but often enough—and maybe he was smelling some of that. But that too would be dried. Besides, some of that kind of smell could be coming from the damp plaster. And the plumbing in a place like this wouldn't be in the best repair.

Old observation, very trite: All dead bodies are the same, yet every one is different.

And no, should a reporter ask, you never really get used to it. . .

He had noticed that some posters relieved the stained wall on the stairway coming up: an announcement of a modern art exhibit with a sample of the art, and another of a rock concert—both long past—and at the top of the staircase, where the light was a little brighter, a stylized stark black fist holding a stylized black submachine gun under a red ¡VENCEREMOS! Well, it was logical—the city branch of the state university was not far, rooms for students and young staff might be cheap around here, and include as well something of what *his* generation had called the Bohemian Life—with drugs added. He sighed ... His generation was so remote that to today's students it must seem legendary. And how could a long-time homicide detective, of all people, remember or understand what it was like to be that young?

He checked the body out, self-consciously professional. ('How many bodies have you seen, sir, in your long career?' 'Sorry. Never kept count ... but mention a name or description, and I'll remember.') The dried blood, the degree of rigor mortis, meant that the man—or boy—had been killed hours before. That wound on the side of the head indicated that death was not due to a fall or other accident—though Birge would wait for the PM results before stating that positively in his report. And estimates about time of death would have to wait on what he got, personally and in writing, from Haskell Collender, chief medical examiner (Birge didn't quite trust the assistants), but it did not seem logical that the boy had been killed before dark. (And did it seem logical at all that he could have been killed without somebody noticing in this wide-open hall, with people passing in and out, probably all night?)

There were few lights—either the

2

superintendent or landlord was trying to save money and he or she did not come around often enough to change burned-out bulbs—so Birge took the flashlight from one of the two precinct cops standing around, squatted down with some difficulty, and shone it on the face and head. They seemed to jump out of the shadow—brown dried blood on the temple and cheek, eyes dulled but staring, teeth— almost perfect teeth—revealed because the lips were drawn back in pain or a beginning cry . . . *My God, he looks like a high school kid . . .* The body was on its side and the knees were drawn up—probably also a reflex to pain, but Birge had seen that fetal position before. *No,* he told the imaginary reporter, *you don't get used to it.*

The sound of his own voice reassured him. 'Get some more light in here. And if they're not already on the way, get on the horn and make sure the ME people and the van— fingerprint, photographer—are notified. What about my office—was it called?'

Birge had picked up the dispatcher's code on his radio, in his own car, while on the way home after about a twenty-hour day. That was why he had come himself, and why he wasn't sure homicide had been alerted.

The patrolman was a little unnerved by having to face the head of a division directly.

To him Birge was a great and powerful man, who could probably break him if he wasn't careful . . . Perhaps because he was so tired, a quotation from his brief stay in college thirty years before swam up into Birge's mind, something about how a great man should be treated as a cross between a willful child and a wild beast. (Who had said that?)

The beast growled: 'Well?'

'Uh, no sir. You see, I was waiting until the precinct detectives came out . . . we notified them, sir.'

Well, that was reasonable in a sense. Patrolmen were supposed to wait for the precinct detectives . . . even if, at this hour, with recent budget cuts, none might be on duty or in the station. If they felt they were being watched or checked on, these cops weren't likely to go over the heads of immediate superiors no matter how long they kept the body and the witnesses waiting. What did he expect? He knew that bureaucracy had to come first.

Birge started to rise, felt a stab in his lower back, and finished more slowly, his left palm on the sore spot—as though that pressure could cancel years, heaviness, and overwork.

He said, 'What's your name?'

The patrolman gave a slight start—now he must be really scared. 'Corporal Shepak, sir.'

4

'All right, Shepak—corporal—you call headquarters, extension 2650—all right, just tell the dispatcher to get homicide—and say Captain Birge wants to know if Lieutenant Hagen called in. And when he does . . . or if he did . . . ' Birge had to pause to take a deep breath. 'Tell them to make sure he gets this address and gets out here.'

He could imagine what Charley Hagen would say—or think—if, after waiting all those years for the old man to retire, he saw Birge holding his back after a 'routine' examination of a corpse.

All right. Let Charley get at least part of his wish—come on out and take over this case. Maybe work twenty hours instead of the sixteen he got away with . . . I'm tired, Birge thought, I want to go home. A pause in routine examinations . . .

Shepak made a pass at a salute and began to leave. Birge called after him: 'Now repeat: What are you going to tell them?'

Again Shepak started. 'I'll tell them to call Lieutenant Hagen and say to report out here, to this address.'

Birge sighed again. 'That's not exactly what I said! Oh all right, let it go.' He turned away. Might do Hagen some good at that, though he couldn't help feeling a little sorry for him. 'And don't forget about the van and the
5

medical examiner.' Do I have to explain everything to these boneheads? Not the same high-class personnel they used to get in your time, eh, Captain Birge?

It was a strain, not only physical, to get back down close to the floor again with the corpse. Really as young as he had appeared? Or, these days, did everybody look like a kid to him? The curly brown hair, no gray; the smooth skin, no wrinkles. Faint lines under the eyes, but that could be from fatigue (studying hard?) or, for that matter, the markings of death. Chino pants, tweed jacket, what looked like a button-down light blue shirt; no tie, naturally. Birge hadn't kept up with modern styles (another point of criticism—the 'elderly gentleman' might easily miss important clues and motives), but even if the boy were some time beyond high school he was still quite young ... despite that scar on his cheek ...

Looked something like Roy Birge had, about the time he started college.

Birge reached carefully and patted the pockets he could reach on the corpse, but the inside breast pocket was caught and held rigid under the left arm, and the wallet would be in the left rear pocket, under the hip.

He asked the remaining patrolman, 'Did you touch the body?'

6

'No sir.'

'Took nothing at all from around it?'

'No sir. Been waiting for instructions.'

Birge nodded. The man *could* have collected some information without jeopardizing the investigation. But ... always encourage following regulations.

'Know who he is?'

'No sir.'

'All right.' They had waited this long, the youth could remain anonymous a little longer. They would wait until the ME's men had finished and the area had been photographed. Birge straightened and looked around.

The body was huddled just around the corner from that stairway to the street. Anyone who came up or down that stairway— certainly anyone coming from or going to either of the apartment entrances facing each other on the short butt of the hall to the left— could not have helped seeing the body once it was there. But there were other entrances to the street that could have been used by most of those from the other apartments, all to the right. It was a rather strangely shaped hallway in an unusual building. The ground floor, on a hill, was given over to glassed small shops and offices—a corner drugstore, a real estate office, a small avant-garde bookshop, a darkened little restaurant or bar—and there

7

were two other staircases. The ostensible front of the building faced Broad St., on the edge of the movie district, but most of its length passed swiftly downhill on Evergreen St., by the stairway entrances, toward slums. Because of the hill and the way the building had been constructed, the apartment doors were at different heights sometimes, often a step or two, from the hall, and in the middle of the length of the hall there were also rising steps. It reminded Birge of the setting for some postwar spy movie in Germany or Austria. From where he stood, it was difficult to see many of the farthest doors.

The university, then the theaters, then this place. A two-bit Greenwich Village should do fine here. Even the slums might lend atmosphere.

It seemed to him improbable that those doors hid people so innocent and untroubled that they could sleep deeply through a murder and the heavy feet and voices of policemen in the hall. He took the long flashlight from the patrolman and swung its beam suddenly along the doors that the beam could reach. One closed quickly. Number 17. He made a mental note, then shut off the light. He would check later.

Pointing to the doors to the left of the stairway, he said, 'Who lives there?'

'It's that studio, sir.'

'What studio?'

'That artist—you know, sir, the one that runs that bar downstairs.'

He didn't know. But Corporal Shepak had said something about people being detained in the bar downstairs, and how he had told them to wait until the detectives came. Birge had been preoccupied with the body, and had not paid enough attention. Another failing.

That twisted body still absorbed him... Unlike some people, including, occasionally, detectives, he had never confused the unconscious with the dead. These days, of course, he had to attend more and more funerals, out of respect to relatives and old colleagues, or to keep Edna company; if the coffin were open and the undertaker had earned his money, someone was sure to say in his hearing, 'Doesn't he look natural? Just like sleep.' Birge usually grunted something like an assent, but he never believed it.

'They still there?'

'Yes sir. Mulvaney would be down there with them.'

Far off he heard a siren. Finally ... and, of course, they had to sound it at four in the morning, as though the body were on fire. And, of course, they would alarm the witnesses and wake the whole street.

9

'You stay here. Watch those doors. Get the names of everybody coming or going. And nobody touches the body before the ME people. That includes photographers, print men, *and* your precinct detectives.'

Birge got downstairs just as the big sedan swept to the curb, the siren muttering its final threats. No identification on the black car, except the lights and that siren. He could almost hear Hagen: Maybe they want the winos to think they're FBI.

Corporal Shepak, apparently having finished calling in, met them. Two plainclothesmen thrust themselves out the car doors. Birge said, 'Cut that noise!'

They looked up. Obviously they couldn't see him clearly against the dark of the doorway, because the young one said, 'Who the hell are you?'

'Homicide. *Captain* Birge. I won't ask your name. Just get upstairs, get the names of any possible witnesses you find awake, and make sure nobody lifts that body until the ME man finishes his initial examination. You'—he pointed to the older plainclothesman—'follow me. And later I'll want a written report about why it took you so long to get here.' Actually, he had no direct authority to order such a report; he was supposed to complain to Harry Harrison, the chief of detectives, who would

10

then order it. He wouldn't bother. He just wanted to keep them on their toes.

'Yessir,' the young man said in a suddenly subdued voice, and went quickly upstairs, making the beginning of a salute as he passed. The other also touched a forefinger to his hat and moved closer to Birge. Shepak—who, without other orders, should have gone upstairs—likewise stayed close.

The nightclub or bar—once a small shop of some kind—had standard plate glass across its front, ending in a door to the left. The bottom half of the glass was blocked out by uneven rectangles that seemed to be the backs of large paintings. Dusty cabaret curtains on a long brass pole hung above them; above that, in an uneven arc—drawn freehand and rather crudely, but therefore perhaps more artistically for all he knew—the name: PETIT MONTMARTRE. Inside the arc were some smaller letters from a language that did not use the Latin alphabet, at least not entirely. But there were few lights shining on or directly behind the glass, so Birge could see little clearly, particularly since the glass had not been cleaned recently.

But the old store was not deep, and at the back, behind an ill-fitting partition and a door, he could see lights and hear indistinct voices. One voice was full, like an actor's, and

11

accented; another, answering it, was a policeman's. (A further skill of an older cop: No matter how they varied, he could almost always tell a policeman's voice, a policeman's walk.)

The door was locked. He motioned to Shepak, who he supposed had a key. Shepak simply took over the rattling, with more vigor, and for good measure gave the frame a kick, causing the glass to pound dangerously. The accented voice shouted something indignant. The far door opened, and a policeman's figure peered out, calling over its shoulder that everyone should stay exactly where they were. 'Open up, Mulvaney!' Shepak shouted, and the figure came forward and turned the knob to release a simple spring lock.

Obviously, Birge thought, they don't keep much money here. Or don't really know the neighborhood. Or are confident the locals wouldn't want to steal anything they have.

Birge's eyes became accustomed quickly to the deeper dimness inside. He had never seen this place before, nor many like it, but it seemed instantly familiar—broad, bare floor planks; tables covered with white-and-red checked tablecloths jammed too close together; old wine bottles on each table so encrusted with candle wax as to look like souvenirs from caves. The candles were out

12

now—when the customers were gone, electricity was apparently cheaper.

He moved rapidly, dodging between the tables. The walls were lined with paintings. He couldn't see them clearly in the shadows, but most seemed to be from the same artist, or at least the same school—stark, smoke-obscured factories and streets, gray landscapes with grayer fog—a realism not much different from what he remembered, indistinctly, from his boyhood.

Or perhaps this was because he saw them in darkness. The door to the kitchen suddenly opened and a yellow beam fell on a dented espresso maker and a row of mugs on the back wall, close to the opening; on the one painting the beam hit he thought he saw sunlight, as yellow and surrounded by shadow as the beam itself . . . Then he and the three policemen had crowded into that little kitchen—no-nonsense, grease-spotted, fluorescent overhead—and stood jammed together, beefy, dark suited, and blinking.

For the time of night, and for its size, that kitchen already held a surprising number of people. The 'civilians' were seated uncomfortably around a battered table, trying to find space for their elbows between stained cutting boards, bowls, and a small chopping block. At the head of the table, as though

13

gravity had naturally pulled him there, sat a heavy, dark man about forty—with strong features just beginning to be softened with fat. His straight, thick black hair fell down almost all the way to his wide, white, Lord Byron collar. He had a theatrical, thick mustache. Probably born in Europe, Birge thought, south or east. He was angry, maybe a little apprehensive. His narrowed eyes quickly checked out the men who had come in, then fixed and stayed on Birge. He was angry, but he waited.

Next to him a slender, rather tall woman was seated. She was in a bathrobe with a scarf over her head—apparently she had been called from sleep, so she must live upstairs. Her face was handsome and olive, the eyes large and dark, but the expression was a little rigid and she held the bathrobe tightly. She was probably no more than thirty—a little young, perhaps, by American standards, for the man next to her, who seemed obviously to be her husband or lover. They sat close, but Birge noted that, though the time must have been tense for both of them, they did not touch nor hold hands.

'I am Captain Birge.' He nodded to Shepak, the senior officer of those who had been first on the scene. His eyes flicked quickly, while he waited for the introductions, to the less

14

striking of those at the table: a frightened-looking waitress, very young; a bent, gray, rather dirty man, probably the cook and responsible for the grease-spattered stove (he made a mental note to have the health department check the place out); and a young man, probably the last patron or a boyfriend of the waitress ... His eyes caught on the youth, then went back to Shepak as he started to speak.

'This is Cap'n Birge from police headquarters,' Shepak said. He paused a moment to let that sink in, ignoring the fact that Birge had already introduced himself. The aura of having a division chief on the scene reflected on him as well as on the importance of the occasion. 'And Cap'n, this gentleman is ...'—he consulted a notebook—'... Mr. ... Mirko Brodovic. He owns this place. And he has an apartment right overhead, upstairs.' Shepak gestured.

'Studio,' the man said. His voice was deep. The accent seemed to be more in the way he inflected his words than in pronunciation.

Shepak looked up. 'What?'

'Studio. That's mostly where I work ... the paintings. The best light.'

'Don't you sleep there too?'

Brodovic half shrugged, lifted a palm.

Shepak looked at Birge. 'He has, I guess,

15

his own entrance. That's a small back stairway or fire escape or something around the back that goes right up to his place.'

Birge hadn't known that. He made a mental note, agreeably surprised that Shepak had found that and recognized its significance. It meant that anyone could have gone up or down that stairway without passing the body or being noticed by the policemen or, for that matter, witnesses on the street. Maybe there was hope for the young cops after all.

'Where and what is it, exactly?'

Shepak gestured toward a small back door that seemed to lead to a foyer and then to the alley. 'I guess it's an inside fire escape. Goes up that back wall.'

Birge remembered now that he had noted a small utility door in the far corner of the hall above, but had assumed it led to a supply closet or the like... Slipping, eh? He nodded to Shepak. 'Thanks.'

To Brodovic he said, 'How long have you been here?'

The man spread his palms. 'All night. This is my restaurant. Where else?'

Birge shrugged. 'Painting, maybe.'

'I paint by daylight. North light. I never use artificial light.' He gestured to indicate the obvious. 'How can you trust colors?'

'You haven't been upstairs at all?'

16

'Once to change a shirt.'

'When?'

'Who knows? Early, maybe ten o'clock.'

'You didn't notice anything strange upstairs?'

'No. What?'

'You don't know why you're here?'

Again the raised palms. 'No. These policemen talk—there's a man—something—upstairs. Something bad happened. I ask them what.' The palms spread. Birge noted that they were broad—thick palms, workmen's hands—but there were no calluses on them. 'They don't tell me anything. "Wait till the detectives come."'

He had been wrong to stop, Birge thought... When he was this tired, it was too easy for him to be rubbed raw. He was sliding into an irritation that was next door to anger. 'You have no idea, huh?' He turned to the woman. 'And this lady?'

'No, Captain.' Her voice was husky—a little slurred, but calm and slow. Her eyes were on him. Her head—with that ridiculous scarf that must hide hair curlers, or something like that—straightened and lifted, queenlike. 'Why are we being kept here?' If there was an accent it was that of the West End, the large stone houses set far back beyond old trees, lawns, fences, and curved driveways.

17

'Your name, please.'

'Jeanne De Plaissy.'

Birge did not usually read society news, and murders in the West End, though they commanded the headlines, did not fill many files in his department. Still, he had heard the name, or ones like it. He motioned toward the painter. 'You're not married to this gentleman?'

'I keep my professional name.'

She had not really answered the question, but he let that pass.

'That's with the double-N and E?'

'Yes . . . Captain, again, why are we here?'

Fatigue kept him from thinking clearly, but did not stop impressions. The whole conversation suddenly seemed insane. There was a body upstairs—somebody who may have been visiting them, whom they might know—a body that she, at least, must have seen in that grim hallway.

He said to her, 'What brought you downstairs?'

She spoke deliberately—not quite as though speaking to a child, but close enough. 'I heard the noise in the hall. The policemen—heavy shoes, the voices. I slipped out and came down that back staircase.' He stared at her. 'Well—I just saw them standing there, so I came the other way, to ask Mirko what was

18

happening. Well, I couldn't go outside like this, could I?'

'You don't seem to have shown much curiosity. And you went the one way the policemen couldn't see you.' He had seen that hall—they should have seen her anyhow, had they been alert. He would find out why not later, but that was another matter.

She had, apparently, become the spokeswoman for the group. 'Well, Captain, if it was a drunken brawl—something like that—well, I didn't think I should be stopped in my nightdress for something that didn't concern us. I thought they would know down here. Is there anything wrong with that?'

He was silent. The black stove attracted his attention again—that and the long row of bottles of seasonings and condiments with strange labels on the streaked shelf above it. When that stove was on, in this close room, the atmosphere must have been stifling... He used the pause to try to get his perceptions organized. He was missing something.

'Sir, I know it doesn't pay to offend the police. But you know you can't detain us here without a warrant or a charge. I believe that's right, isn't it?' the woman asked.

'I can for a capital crime. There is a dead man in the hall, on the landing at the top of this first staircase that runs up alongside this place.' He pointed his thumb toward the stairway. 'He lies on the side toward the end of the hall. There are only two doorways close ... pardon me—three. That busy fire escape. I forgot that one.'

He watched them for reactions. Brodovic's face grew dark. One hand gripped the end of the table. Birge thought he started a harsh glance toward the woman, but he couldn't be sure because it was as though the man knew he was being watched and brought himself under complete control very quickly. A dangerous man, Birge decided. But probably not when he knew he wouldn't win.

The cook simply looked frightened. He had, no doubt, worked in places before in which there occasionally was sudden death and disturbance, and had learned to try to look for somewhere to hide; his eyes now seemed to be searching for such a place. The young man at the end of the table gave a sudden start, and Birge turned toward him a second and caught his startled eye. This delayed his concentration on the woman.

Her hand had gone to her throat. She had gone almost completely white. She said, 'Dead? A dead man?'

Birge asked, 'Did you think he wasn't?'

'I didn't know.' She whispered it. 'I didn't know that's why the police were there.'

20

'You did see them, then. Why did you think they were there?'

Her lips seemed to move a little before she was audible. 'I didn't know. So many things . . . happen in this neighborhood.'

'It's a disgrace!' Brodovic said. 'It's not safe even in your own building. Just last week, two people were robbed upstairs. We don't know who's going to come into the hall. A drunk last week! Why can't we get protection?'

Because the police are Philistines, Birge thought. An unfortunate fact. If we had cops at the door checking everybody that came in or hauling off somebody every time we got a complaint, the screams would reach clear down to City Hall . . . If some of the cops at headquarters had their way, they wouldn't be waiting for warrants to be into every apartment and medicine chest in this place. And the screams would be justified.

'Did you call us about those crimes? We're not a secret police. We can't barge into buildings or apartments without a warrant or a complaint.'

The woman's eyes were still on him. He had half withdrawn his notebook from his pocket. He recognized a familiar grinding of gears as a vehicle shifted down coming around the corner. He put the notebook back. Outside, the van growled as it pulled to the curb. The

21

ME people would be with the van or close behind. He signaled to Mulvaney to go outside. 'Take them straight upstairs.' Then he turned back to the table. 'I'll have to ask you to come upstairs to identify the body, if you can.'

But he was distracted, and failed to see how that affected the woman. The waitress—a young, white-faced girl with straight, long black hair and frightened eyes—suddenly began to cry. 'Oh, please, sir. Why do I have to? I haven't done anything.' Her wet eyes looked toward Brodovic for support. 'I haven't been out of here all night—not even to go to the bathroom—you know that, Mirko...'

So she called her employer by his first name? But did that mean anything? She had a slight accent too. Probably he drew his help from family or friends.

Brodovic took out a pipe and began to stuff tobacco in it. There are advantages to having a droopy mustache like a Balkan mountain guerrilla—it hides enough of the mouth and face, especially when accompanied by lowered eyes, to make the reading of expression difficult. But Birge could see that the apparently unconcerned pipe lighting was not the whole story; the flame, as it was sucked into the bowl, trembled a little. 'She never went upstairs,' he agreed in a flat voice.

'You see, sir; you see, sir? I want to go home!' Her voice rose on each phrase as if on steps.

'I just want identification,' Birge said. He knew that by now the ME men, under the watchful eyes of the policemen he had detailed, had probably already identified the body, or would certainly have done so, if there were any identification cards at all, before he and the others arrived. But he wanted eyewitness corroboration. And he wanted to see who knew that body while it lived, and where and how well. And he wanted to watch the faces.

He sighed tiredly. (I know, I know, too old for these hours.) 'All right,' he told the waitress. 'You won't have to go up yet. I'll call you if I need you.'

The damp lips trembled, but he looked away, finally toward (Miss? Mrs.? Ms.?) De Plaissy. She had had plenty of time to compose her face but it was still without color.

Mulvaney returned and once more Birge nodded to him. To those at the table he said, 'Follow me, please.'

'Please, sir? Sir? Can't I just go home?'

'Only a little longer. I'll have somebody drive you if you're afraid you'll miss a bus.'

The bloodshot eyes of the cook watched

23

him anxiously, though with little hope. In those eyes, and the splotched nose as well as the expression, Birge recognized the marks of the long-time alcoholic. Again he felt a surge of anger against Brodovic. To hire someone like this to prepare food for the public, just because, apparently, he was cheap! Probably drunk most of the time off the job, and sometimes on the job too.

Still, on the other hand... ('The captain always has at least three hands,' he had once heard Hagen complain to a detective who had wanted fast and violent action against a suspect, 'so we have to wait till he figures out which one has the pea.') ... on the other hand, being a drunk did not necessarily make him a bad cook. And would he be better off turned loose on the street?

'I wasn't never out of this kitchen,' the cook offered in a hoarse rumble.

'It looks like it. All right—you stay here till we dismiss you. And clean this place up. Now would the rest follow me, please?'

He did not bother to look at the young man at the end of the table again. He was probably a little older than the body upstairs—and getting older by the second—but there seemed a certain generic resemblance despite differences. Birge could recognize that now. What would young men with jobs, or with a heavy load of schoolwork, be looking for in an imitation Greenwich Village restaurant in the early hours? The obvious answer—that most detectives would immediately accept—was the women. But, while Birge was there, the young man had hardly looked at them and exchanged no conversation.

He would not take that inside stair now; he could explore it later. So they had to go through the dark restaurant, outside, then turn and go through the street door. He led the way, past those posters—which this time he examined more closely—the one of the art exhibit, dramatic swirls of stark color against the spotted greenish plaster and uneven lettering for no particular reason that he could see; the rock concert poster, now curled at the edges and with gray streaks; and the call for Latin American revolutionary movements to conquer, if that's what it was. Then the hall upstairs, brightly lit now, thronged with heavy men gathered in a cluster—a production staged by the police. The photographer had apparently finished; his camera was down and he had become another onlooker. Two ME men were stooped over the body... Birge noticed too that there were three onlookers apparently from the apartments—two women in bathrobes, one with hair curlers, and a youngish man who had pulled on jeans but was barefoot, and with a grayish undershirt. Corporal Shepak, with a notebook, was talking to them.

The examiners had gone through the pockets, but they had not disturbed the body much. It still stared sightlessly, the corner of the slightly open mouth wincing from the long-extinguished pain. The pocket contents were being listed and examined, then placed inside a large brown envelope. The wallet was there, and Birge could see a social security card and what looked like a driver's license, so there would be little trouble about identification. The ME man handed the envelope to him with the wallet separate, but without examining it closely Birge dropped it inside.

One ME man was the familiar white-haired ancient who usually guarded the portals of the morgue like somebody from a Poe movie, and who had been there so long that not even Birge could remember what political hack or committeeman had gotten him his job. But the other, with a ridiculous charcoal jacket over his operating blouse, was one of Haskell Collender's assistants, who had undoubtedly come along at this hour when he picked up the information, which Shepak couldn't repress, that the chief of homicide himself was at the scene. He was a little nervous as he looked up at Birge: Haskell was breezy and casual about police routine with Birge, but not with his own staff. 'Tell us when you want this body removed, sir. We can't do much till we get him to the morgue.'

'Not long.' Birge turned to the photographer. 'You have all you need?'

'Unless you want something in particular, Captain.'

Birge nodded. One of the blessings of technology since he had come on the force was that cameras had become so efficient and trouble-free that he could count on the results if the photographer had any competence at all. 'I'll let you know.'

The man from the van was carrying the fingerprint kit and waiting for instructions, but Birge could think of none offhand. Fingerprints would be useless in a public hall, or on flesh or clothes. They would be useful on the weapon, but only if that could be found.

'What cause?' he asked the ME.

'Can't be sure until after the autopsy and samples have been analyzed, but that blow on the head might be sufficient.'

'That alone?'

'I think so. We've had ones like it, even from falls. Heavy enough instrument, swung hard enough. Spongy bone there. And there's another blow on the back of the head. Probably while he was down.' To illustrate, the ME brought his fist down as though driving a heavy nail with a hammer. 'Get a lot of force that way.' He paused thoughtfully, considering a technical problem. 'Of course can't be sure until we get him on the table.'

A common object, found in every home... And snatched up without much planning. That would narrow the possibilities as to weapon, sequence of events, and even motive and kind of homicide. And they could start looking around immediately in garbage cans and in the area, assuming that the lack of premeditation and planning would carry through when it came to getting rid of the evidence.

But if the weapon had been deliberately chosen, was somehow unique, and therefore there had been planning, that would also narrow their search.

The group behind him had stayed at the top of the stairs, a few steps behind. He had indicated, not very forcefully, that they might remain there a moment while he took care of preliminary business, and they had not argued. They could see the body from there, but not see or hear the details he was discussing. Those who knew the boy, though, should by now see whose body it was.

Birge lowered his voice, leaning down closer to the body. He had not really noticed the blow to the back of the head before. (He had good reasons, of course—he had not wanted to turn the body until the ME men were there, and so on—but that didn't excuse him.)

First, limit the possibilities. Commercial lumber was usually cut on the square, and might leave distinctive marks. 'Could it be wood?'

'Something like a nightstick or baseball bat, maybe. I think something metal might be more likely.' Birge could almost hear Haskell snapping, 'You're not paid to conjecture!' But he was glad to get this unofficial opinion now.

'Pipe?'

'Yes.'

'Hammer?'

'That would certainly do it.' Maybe the young man also now began to hear the voice of the chief medical examiner. 'I don't think I should say anything else about it until the autopsy, sir.' Without Haskell's permission, that is.

Birge nodded once more. But he did not intend to wait. He would leave as soon as Hagen relieved him.

He straightened up and motioned to the three from downstairs. 'Step a little closer, please ... Now. Do you recognize this man? Mr. Brodovic?'

Pipe smoke, combined with a mustache, could make a face quite indistinct. 'I seen him. He's a customer, comes around pretty often. Usually late. Works late or something.'

'His name?'

Brodovic shook his head. 'If I heard I don't remember.'

The woman was next. She knew she would be asked—she would know that there was no point in dissembling, and that to pretend to have no emotion would not be natural—so she could let herself go. A little bit anyway. But it was more than that. Her lips trembled and her hands, white knuckled, wrestled together briefly. She said, 'Oh my God!'

'You know him then,' Birge said. 'What's his name?'

Her eyes clung, starkly fascinated, to the head and face. She muttered something.

'Yes? I'm sorry, I didn't hear that. What did you say?'

'Wes ...' She cleared her throat, took a short breath. 'Yes. I know him. ... His name is Wesley. Wesley Gowen.'

Birge wrote it down. He did not ask about spelling. It somehow did not seem the time to discuss with her whether the last name was spelled with an *e* or an *a*. The wallet and the

30

records would have correct details.

'How well did you know him?'

'He's a boy . . . used to come into the restaurant.'

He waited. 'That's all?' Brodovic had said that much, and he pretended not to know the name.

'We talked often . . . I think I knew him well enough to talk.'

'You never saw him outside the restaurant?'

'There was a small group that used to visit sometimes in my apartment. He became one of them.'

'Talk about what?'

'Art. Life . . . things. What we wanted. Things like that. I think he might have been a talented boy.'

'Do you teach?'

'Only night school, a little. Design and commercial art. That is . . . at the university.'

Just in case he should think it was only high school . . . But that was uncharitable. The night school, of course, at a university in the center of the city was more than twice as large as the day school. Birge would often see the students, many of them middle-aged—and some young ones who had not been able to go to day college—coming out of the buses and the parking lots in streams, surging across the boulevard at the crossings, a restless tide

31

searching in the lighted, imitation Gothic buildings for whatever it was they had missed, or hoped still to achieve. Her classes were probably large.

'Did you meet him there?'

'No. He works. Worked ... he worked late, through the evening hours. He would stop in here after work.' She paused and inhaled, like an inverted sigh, between each sentence. When she stopped speaking he could tell from the rise and fall of her bosom that the jerky breathing continued.

She was standing, none too steadily, in the open hall. Silence had fallen on the group. They were listening to the questioning; they were all watching her. Another question might make her break down in front of all those eyes. Maybe not, but he could not be sure. And he was pretty sure that most of the questions he might ask her now would be answered in the reports on his desk in the morning—afternoon, rather, since it was morning already—the boy's history, where he worked, where he lived, with whom.

She was without sleep and the dead man was at her feet. Hagen might think that now might be the time to put pressure on her, but Birge could not agree. If it really profited them to watch her break down, it could be done in her apartment or his office. She would tell him about the relationship sooner or later.

Another slamming of car doors downstairs. Soon—perhaps after a short delay to ask a patrolman on the sidewalk or in the bar what was up—there would be the now-familiar pounding by heavy men up those stairs. That would be Hagen. He looked around at the faces that had drawn closer to him while he had been questioning the woman. The man with the dirty T-shirt and bare feet seemed particularly avid with curiosity, acting as a kind of pointer for the women close to him, who seemed always waiting for his lead... The police department men, though, when they saw Birge turning toward them, became very busy, looking up later to see if he was still watching.

He heard the feet hitting those stairs. It seemed to him—a sudden relaxing, deep inside—that soon, though the case was just beginning, his day would finally be over.

'That's all for now,' he told her. 'We'll make an appointment later for my office.'

She seemed to be trying to pull her eyes away from the body. Birge put his hand under her arm, and, as though this gave her permission, she turned her head away and stepped back.

Lt. Charley Hagen was at the top of the steps, blinking in the brighter lights that had been set up by the photographer. But he wasn't missing anything; the red eyes swept across those standing, quickly categorized them, then went swiftly for the body... Birge could imagine what that same uncompromising analysis had done to the posters along the stairs.

Hagen, the department dandy, had not taken time to shave, and even his shirt looked as though it might be entering its second day. For some reason that must have been related to the hours he had put in, this gave Birge a perverse satisfaction. 'Sorry to get you out, Charley, but you've been taking it pretty easy lately. Sometimes as much as four hours' sleep.'

Hagen grunted. He was not happy, but he was already interested in the case. And he knew he was supposed to do most of the legwork anyhow. He was at Birge's side, and said, 'What we got?'

Birge briefed him. He pointed out that he had not yet gotten the information from the specialists, the photographer, fingerprint and lab men, nor the details being collected by the precinct detectives. He signaled to Shepak, who came over, notebook at the ready. 'Who are they?'

Shepak consulted the notebook. 'You mean those three.' It was a statement, not a question. The dirty T-shirt, knowing apparently that he was being discussed, was staring at them. 'They live down the hall—'

'Where?'

'Apartment 27. That's over there beyond the steps. They said they came out to see what the noise was about, and came down to investigate.'

'Do they know the victim?'

'I don't think so. The guy said maybe he did, he wasn't sure. The girls said they weren't sure.'

Birge snorted. 'What were they doing up so late?'

'Said they were talking—I don't know, he said about Buddhism, or something like that... That guy—he's pretty much of a wise-ass. Kept trying to ride me. Smells of pot. I got their names here.' He closed the notebook. 'Think I should run them in?'

'Just give their names to Lt. Hagen. We're not out after pot.' The dirty T-shirt, with a half-defiant, half-uneasy smile just above it, was still turned toward him, apparently happy at having won this much attention—and from a police captain at that.

The three civilians he had asked to follow him upstairs were standing close to the stairway, each, separately, shooting glances at the body and then away. The woman was swaying a little; he might not have noticed except that Brodovic put out a hand to steady her, and Birge could see her move toward the body, then start back. He had not asked the young man to view the corpse, and he did not ask him now. 'You three—thanks. Sorry for the inconvenience. Get some rest now, and be in my office at headquarters at one P.M. Better make that two.' Brodovic started to say something about his restaurant, but Birge waved him on and turned back to Hagen, who had raised his eyebrows. 'We can get their evidence later. Just finish up around here and get it on my desk before two. Then I'll take over and you might even be able to get some sleep.'

Brodovic and De Plaissy went to their apartments—right across the hall from one another, Birge observed, the man above his restaurant, the woman directly facing—the two doors closest to the body. The young man went down the stairs. Birge said to Shepak, 'That cook and waitress downstairs—tell them to go home. But get names and addresses.'

He noticed that his legs were a little shaky, and the soles of his feet, as he started down the steps, were rather sore. He paused to rest them, and to stare at the posters, then went on.

On the street, where there should have been

quiet, he heard voices. To his left, perhaps twenty feet away on the rising pavement, Mulvaney was arguing with a man. Between them, behind the row of badly parked police vehicles, a taxi had pulled to the curb, its exhaust white, the driver looking from the cars to the argument with curiosity and a little apprehension. As Birge passed him he called, 'Hey! You ast for a cab?'

'Wait.'

To Mulvaney he said, 'What's the trouble here?'

'These people—they came out of that entrance there.' He pointed to a door between the bookshop and the real estate office, one of those connecting to the hall upstairs, but farther on. 'I was just askin' who they were, what they were doin', and this man here is givin' me a argument.' He shrugged and began to smile. 'I guess—'

'All right,' Birge said.

The man was heavyset, his iron gray hair a little rumpled. He had on a dark tweed jacket—but also leather house slippers over his socks. The woman still had her face turned, but Birge could see that she was crying. She was not a woman, but a girl.

'I don't see why this man stops me,' the man said. 'We—I haven't done anything.'

'What apartment are you from?'

37

'I don't see what right—'

'I'm a police captain, and a crime has been committed. What apartment? And were you visiting or do you live there?'

'Just upstairs. Apartment 17.'

'Oh yes. I saw your door open once. That first stairway is closest to you, but you saw what was there, and went out of your way to come down this one?'

'Well ... well, that's all right, we had nothing to do with that. And I didn't want this lady to be delayed or anything.'

'She a relative of yours?'

'Just one of my students. We had a class tonight and finished late and I didn't have her papers. So she came with me to go over ... some of the material ... But whoever you are, I don't see—'

Birge said to Mulvaney, 'Get his name, and the particulars of where he was, and what he might have seen and heard tonight. No—not the girl. Just let her go home.'

Hagen would have disapproved of that too, so Birge was glad that he had come down first. He signaled peremptorily to the cab driver, whose head had been twisted around so he could watch through the dirty back window. The cab backed up jerkily, old gears whining, and the girl got in. Birge turned and went down the row of vehicles toward his own—the only one properly parked. He had a sudden wild desire to tell Mulvaney to ticket them all. That lightened his mood for about a second.

He heard a familiar voice from the right and glanced through the restaurant window. Brodovic was finally closing the place, and was apparently unhappy that the cook and waitress had started for home when dismissed by the police rather than himself. The perfect proprietor.

Just above the store window, in one of the windows from Brodovic's apartment that would front the street, Birge thought he saw a reflection of a face on the glass. It was a face. The lights in the room were out and it caught only the harsh, attenuated streetlight, so that it seemed to float with no collar or body, white and ghostlike above him. It was, or seemed, small, the features drawn; for a moment it looked down at him, then disappeared. It did not move out, just, apparently, stepped into a zone where the streetlight did not reach.

He started walking again, very conscious of the ache in his legs and the sour taste in his mouth. The street descended slowly but steadily, in the long decline that finally ended in the river. A broad stretch of sky was visible, and a dim gray light was beginning to spread on the rim. As he bent to open his car, an alarm clock went off somewhere above him,

39

ending somebody's dreams.

CHAPTER TWO

'His name is—or was—Wesley Gowen,' Birge said. His listeners, Hagen and Haskell Collender, both knew that, of course. But the way to start a report, even an informal oral one, is with the facts. 'He lived with his mother, Matilda Gowen. She is a widow. They have a small house in Overland Hills that his father first bought—took a mortgage on—about ten years ago, a couple of years before he died.'

'Did you talk to the mother?' Collender asked.

'No.' He had called in instructions to send out a particular, older policewoman to break the news to her, talk to her, get background information. He had once asked the chief whether they couldn't hire trained social caseworkers—give them police rank if necessary—to do jobs like that, but that had been dismissed as another one of old Birge's strange ideas. But he couldn't complain—the policewoman had done a good job—while probably wondering why she was never allowed to work full-time as a detective, and about 'status' and 'role.'

'Well,' Haskell said, 'I expect she'll be coming around to my office.'

Unless asked for a specific purpose, the chief medical examiner had no business in Birge's office now, on the first conference and rehash of information on a case, but he usually came anyway, sometimes to contribute insights that his written reports couldn't include, or to listen. Birge suspected he often came just for relief or to drink Edna's coffee— Birge brought a thermos with two cups to start the day before he had to rely on whatever it was that was brewed in the outer room. Collender usually got away with one cupful, cheerfully insulting it all the while. Overall, though, Birge was glad to have him. But he was annoyed at being interrupted. 'I'm sure it won't be for your company.'

Hagen was walking up and down the office slowly, smoking, covering the whole lower half of his face with his cupped hand each time he brought the cigarette to his mouth. He had been relieved and could have gone home— should have gotten more sleep—but he was waiting to hear Birge summarize the case, probably to see if there were some fact, in combination with other material, that might give him an angle. He seldom volunteered, often complained, usually was critical, but he was almost always there when needed. He paused to glance with reddened eyes from one to the other. 'That the whole family?'

'There's supposed to be a brother—another son—somewhere. He tried to support them a while, then pulled a stint in the army. The mother saved as much of her allotment as she could. He got out, took the money, then went west. Gone. She doesn't have his address. Wesley was her chief support.' Would she be able to keep that 'little house' now? Move on to the next fact. 'He worked at the U.S. Package Service. Taking in packages, loading trucks. That big barn on Ninth St. Since he had practically no seniority—he started part-time two years ago, and has been working full-time only since last January—he usually pulled the swing shift, sometimes the night shift.' Birge spread out the papers on his desk like a huge poker hand, squinted through his reading glasses until he found the right one, and moved his finger to the item. Something a policewoman would have been more likely to pick up than, say, Connelly or Rodigault. 'His mother was very proud that he got that job. Jobs are hard to get, especially for kids not long out of high school, no experience, but he got it, passed hard tests. Ambitious boy. Going to night school. When he could get time off . . . Mother says.'

42

Hagen's expression, the way he looked at Birge over his cupped hand, said that he was very tired, not only from work but of irrelevancies. 'That what he was doing in that joint, night after night?'

'We don't know how often,' Birge said. 'Could be stopping in on way home from work, day or swing shift.' But Hagen was right: Mama obviously didn't have the whole story.

'Didn't Judy ask about that?' Hagen usually referred to policemen by their last names, but policewomen always by first names, even those with superior rank.

'No.' She might have felt that the same session in which a mother was told that her son was dead was not the time also to grill her about unwelcome secrets about that same son ... True, many besides Hagen could point out that the best time to get information from people was when they were most vulnerable ... he had done that himself.

He was still too tired to think about it much. 'We can check back with her later. We have better sources to find out what he was doing after hours.' Of course the mother would know Wesley wasn't coming straight home. She probably waited up for him. Probably—he didn't know her, but he didn't think she would be very different from Edna

43

or any other 'respectable' mother—she would have mentioned it to him. And the son may have told her to mind her own business... Although, from her description in the report, it was more likely that he had lied, or simply said that he was stopping for coffee or a beer on the way home, and was entitled, wasn't he? Birge had a son, and Hagen did not; firsthand experience had some advantages even for policemen who went by the book. Edna Birge would have decided that, after a few mysterious absences and some evasions, it was time to have a 'serious talk' with the boy... And, as he remembered, that hadn't worked out so well either. And Mrs. Gowen didn't have a police captain to back up her decisions...

'He isn't registered at the state university, not the city branch. He did register over a year ago, but had to drop out, he said because of work schedules. They remember him because he had trouble getting his money back. American Literature and Creative Writing. De Plaissy does teach there, night school. One class in commercial art. He was never in her class.'

He moved quickly through the stapled reports. 'No criminal record.' He paused a moment, his finger on the sheet. There had been a drunken and reckless driving charge for a group of teenagers after a high school graduation party, but Wesley Gowen hadn't been the driver. Disturbing the peace because he had argued with the cop, but that was dismissed. Birge decided not to mention it. 'Looks pretty clean. Not our usual clientele.'

'Victims can include the best people,' Collender said.

Homicide had to face the frequent charge that they discriminated, spending more time and resources investigating the deaths of the rich than the poor, the white than the black, the newsworthy than the insignificant. Birge always resented the charge, but he had to discriminate in a different sense because he had to choose and allocate according to what was more important, more efficient, or closest to the orders he got from the chief. With all the work they had to do, was this case worth tying up the two top men, himself and Hagen, for even a few days? Would the killer be hard to find? Would he—or she—if not stopped, strike again soon—the ultimate test of whether a case was important?

Birge said, 'Haskell, what's your report? Anything unusual?'

'Preliminary report is right there.' Collender jabbed at it. 'Final one when specimens are analyzed and I get a chance to dictate it.'

45

'You can't dictate it because you're sitting here drinking my coffee. And you didn't dictate—don't you ever write?—that one either. I already talked to your assistant. Now I want something personal from you, based on experience from all the years you been drawing pay here. Anything catch your eye? What's unusual?'

'What's to tell? Healthy young man. Slender, reasonably well muscled, I guess from that job. I don't see any trace of drugs, anything like that, though we don't have the last word. Looks like an accident victim, not a murder. Part of the Sunday morning service.' While other offices were closed on Sunday morning and other men went to church or slept late, the police and the morgue were dealing with the results of the Saturday night drunken fights and auto accidents. For some reason these bodies seemed to bother Collender more than the others—so many had been young and healthy. 'Lord! Well, that major wound—not very big, actually. Concentrated on a small area.'

'Round area?'

'Not clear. Some bone splinters and so on. But it could have been.'

'Not a bullet?'

'No, nothing like that. Anyway, we didn't find any, and there was no exit wound.'

Birge nodded. He had seen enough wounds to know that neither of those visible to him on the body was from a bullet—nor a knife—but it was convenient to have science back up his judgment, and prevent future criticism.

The medical examiner took his gum-soled shoes off Birge's scarred desk and carefully put his empty cup in their place. 'By the way, Sam.' His voice became dry and precise, as though he were dictating that final report. 'That boy had mastoiditis.'

'When he died?'

'No. I would guess nine or ten years ago.'

'Was he operated on for it?'

'Oh no. Hardly done these days, Sam ... you're from a different generation. But it did go pretty far before they caught it. Kid must have been pretty sick. Wonder why. Out of carelessness, probably.'

Birge thought of that mother. 'I doubt carelessness. Lack of money, maybe fear. Why is this relevant?' Collender liked to kid around, but when he talked that way, in that dry voice, he had a purpose.

'Some necrosis. In the days before antibiotics he would have been in pretty bad shape. Anyway, that bone was weakened.'

'That side blow was directly on the mastoid?' Collender looked at him, sucking on his brush mustache. Birge's voice became half

47

apologetic, and he didn't want it to. 'The blood had run. And I didn't want to disturb anything before your man got there.'

Collender nodded, working on that lip, as though he had been thinking of something else all the time. 'Uh-huh.'

'Would a piece of pipe have done it?'

'Probably not if it landed flat, or even. But full swing, one end first . . . quite possibly.'

'But more likely something like a hammer?'

'With leverage, yes. Not necessarily, of course. I have sent blood samples and tissue from the wound for more analysis.' He sighed. 'Sort of a hard-luck kid.'

Birge looked at him a moment. Hagen had stopped his pacing and stood at the edge of the desk. 'What you're saying,' Birge said carefully, 'is that that particular kind of instrument, with that force, at that angle, on that weakened bone . . .'

Collender too sat silent and motionless for perhaps three seconds, then nodded.

'Then . . .' Birge said, still carefully, 'then the blow did not, probably, need to have been struck by a man . . . or anybody very strong. Or with much skill.'

'If it hit . . . happened to hit . . . just right.'

'Yes. Just right. Happened.'

'Of course we're just conjecturing.'

'Yes.'

48

Pause. Then Collender repeated, 'Hard luck.'

'Not up to us to decide.'

'Well, you have to hunt the guilty party. Alleged guilty.'

This was one of Collender's favorite themes in these conferences that he used for needling sessions, and Birge didn't want to discuss it anymore. Who is guilty? What degree and what dividing line? And if you do catch him, will that diminish crime or help the victim?

By implication, what did that boy's death—and Birge's life work—mean?

What business was any of that of the medical examiner's office anyhow! 'Haskell, just give us the information we ask for—or what you in your wisdom think important—will you? Nobody appointed me judge and jury, and they certainly didn't appoint you.'

Collender became abruptly alert and sober-faced. 'All right, Sam. No offense or criticism intended . . . I must say I just don't envy your job.'

'All right . . . I don't think I'd like cutting corpses either.' He managed a smile.

'Takes all kinds to make law enforcement, *n'est-ce pas?*'

'Yes, yes. I don't want to discourage that extra mile you sometimes put in, so please let us know what else comes up, even if it's as far off the left field wall as most of your comments.'

Hagen had moved close during their interchange, and was standing stiffly at the side of his desk. 'You wanted to say something, Charley?'

Hagen started to speak, but had to stop to clear his throat twice before he could go on. 'I didn't see any evidence that it was an accident.'

'What did I miss?' Birge asked.

'Well, I looked all around. He didn't get that wound from any fall, or anything like that.' He took a deep breath and cleared his throat again. Lord, Birge thought, I wish he'd sleep a few hours now. 'That wasn't any accident.'

'You think there might have been some kind of fight?' That was the classic argument for plea bargaining for manslaughter two: The victim and the killer had gotten into an argument over a woman, a fancied insult, a baseball score, anything—and the killer happened to hit faster and harder ... and 'just right'—but he didn't mean to kill at all ... If there were no reliable willing eyewitnesses and the lawyer was competent and well paid, he might be expected to try to take it a step further—if the killer hadn't struck that blow, in desperation, he could

50

have been the victim. Self-defense, your honor.

'What weapon? There weren't any other bruises on his face and—I bet—his body. None on his knuckles. Even if he'd seen that weapon coming in time to throw up his arm— even if he'd only deflected it to another spot— from what you say he could've lived. But no mark on that arm. And the position. He went down like he was poleaxed. From that angle— that angle'—Hagen pointed a slightly shaky finger at Collender—'that angle you talked about—where did that blow come from? Over his shoulder, didn't it? From the side, or behind. If the killer faced him—wouldn't he do something? Never even ducked, or raised his arm. Like he was poleaxed!'

'Well, we'll have to get all our facts together, but so far that seems logical,' Collender said cautiously. When speaking to Hagen, in this mood, he was always cautious. 'All I'm saying is, in most other circumstances, that blow would probably not have been fatal.'

Hagen's reddened eyes stayed on Collender—as though he expected him to make excuses, to get a killer off, to make their work impossible. 'You want to get to intent? Probably waiting . . . coming up behind . . .'

'Assault that results in death—law's pretty

51

clear on that in this state, Haskell,' Birge said. 'Anyway, it's not up to us to decide the charge.' Certainly not up to the medical examiner. 'Let's leave that to the prosecutor.'

'Even if he's a prep and Ivy League idiot,' Hagen said.

Collender laughed and raised his empty cup, and the tension was past. 'All right then, men. Carry on. I'll call you later.'

'Thanks, Haskell... Charley, why don't you take off too? I can handle these interrogations.'

'I'll just hang around a little longer. Just a little.' He allowed himself a yawn, and rubbed the back of his head. 'Pretty tired.'

'Aren't we all.' Birge glanced at his wristwatch—he still couldn't get used to these digital things—and dialed the outer office. 'All right. Apologize for the delay and send in the man—Brodovic—first.' He would give the least information, so might as well get him out of the way. 'Tell the other two they won't have to wait long.'

In the moment before the door opened again he leaned back in his creaking wooden swivel and looked out his window at the two old trees, now in full leaf, left after the recent expansion that had increased the parking lot and added an addition to the morgue.

CHAPTER THREE

Brodovic had put on a jacket and apparently something—probably water—to hold his hair down. Though he wore no tie and still had that Lord Byron collar—its ends tucked tidily inside the jacket—his appearance seemed considerably altered: smaller and more solid, as though fitted into and held by a frame; the successful Slavic businessman, perhaps an importer of ethnic foods and goods, preserver of old-country customs and art, although very American and up-to-date.

'Sorry if you were kept waiting,' Birge said. 'Sit down, please.'

Brodovic nodded and sat on the chair at the side of the desk, half facing Birge. His eyes touched the old desk, the institutional green walls that had needed painting for at least three years, the tattered notices, and the dusty rubber plant, and then came to rest, watchfully, on Birge's face. He had drawn some conclusions—probably shrewd but wrong ones—about Birge's competence and authority. But, also, he was waiting to learn more before taking any chances.

'Now that the dead man has been identified, especially so clearly by Miss'—he

53

glanced at the sheets before him but they did not have a Mrs. in front of the name—'De Plaissy, I wonder if you can't remember more about him.'

'First, sir, I would like to say ... I'm very, very sorry for the young man. I'm very, very sorry this happened. Believe me, this kind of thing never happened before ... close to my place. It's a quiet place, educated people. We study, talk about art together—'

'I know this hasn't happened there in recent years. We keep records here, and I've already checked.' He glanced down at the other's broad hand, which held the corner of the desk in a tight—but not noticeably nervous—grip. 'Just answer the question, please.'

'Well, I know him by sight. Yes, he would come in once in a while, say hello. He never bought much.'

'Did he come in alone?'

'Usually, I think. Take up a whole table. Sometimes he sat with others. He had some kind of friends, or meet somebody—you know. I think he came with girls a few times. Once with a pretty one. That was early in the evening.' He nodded, remembering the girl at least.

'But you didn't remember the name.'

'Well, I don't know the names of most of the people who come in. A few, of course.

They come to see my paintings, or to learn about art, or good food. It's a nice place to come, artists, students. Sort of a ... European place. I talk to them about my work, the meaning of art. You know.'

And they better not disagree, Birge thought. Sitting there, with that tight coat, Brodovic looked more like the bouncer. But then, examining those distempered walls, he turned his profile to Birge, the head held back. Without asking permission he had lit a cigarette; a blue thread of smoke rose and coiled gracefully about his head. It was a good profile. Portrait of the artist.

'Some are serious students. You know. They come in. See the paintings.' He gestured largely. 'They want to ... find out.'

'Students from the university?'

'Yes. And from all over ... I know it doesn't *look* like much, sir—but the Montmartre is well-known these days.'

Somehow Wesley Gowen had been shoved aside in this discussion about Brodovic's art. Birge had never heard of him, but homicide detectives were not notoriously art buffs. He glanced up at Charley Hagen, hovering over both of them from the opposite side of the desk like some sort of dark cloud, insisting that they get back to business—business as Hagen defined it, which had nothing to do with art. About crime and the places it occurred, Hagen had a memory like a computer bank's, and he might have heard of Brodovic, the building, the neighborhood, in ways that Birge had not. That would come out in their later discussions. But might not art, even Brodovic's, have had something to do with Gowen's life—and death?

'Was Wesley Gowen one of your students?'

'Well ... there are many ... some every day.' He got off the dead man pretty quickly. 'Please understand me, sir. I am not a teacher. I do not conduct regular classes. If people, young people, want to come ... you know.'

The natural harshness of Hagen's voice was aggravated by what was an apparently developing sore throat: 'Didn't you know that kid well enough to talk to?'

'Well, of course I talk to many—'

'I'm not asking about that. That kid used to come there pretty regular. We know that already. He knew you, I'm pretty sure. And he died right outide your apartment, right upstairs from your restaurant. And you've been doing a lot of thinking about it. So quit spreading that crap around that you didn't know him!'

'But I don't know—'

'Let's try this: Was there a fight or anything like that—argument over a girl or a ballgame,

56

two beered-up college kids pushing each other and being told to take it outside?'

'There was never a fight! Believe me, never in my place—'

'We got a rusty medal on the wall over there for the only joint in this city that never had a fight . . . All right. Some guys maybe had an argument, they went, or you sent them, out to fight it out somewhere else; or it's possible that Gowen went upstairs to get away and somebody or more than one person followed him. You couldn't help that, could you? Come on, come on—let's make it easy on everybody. This ain't the Kennedy assassination!'

'Nothing—nothing like that ever happened! Where do you get your ideas?' His voice had gone up. His eyes looked more anxious at the same time that his face tried to look more stubborn.

He turned to Birge. Time for the good detective now to come into the act to offer support and understanding in return for the same cooperation that the bad detective was demanding . . . Birge frowned, but he did take over the questioning.

'We've been talking about your restaurant. But that's not where Wesley Gowen died. What was he doing upstairs? Was he going to see someone?'

Brodovic let out a measured breath: some

relief, but not much. 'I don't know. A lot of people live up there. They move in and out.'

'Can you think of any in particular? You might have seen him with them in the restaurant, for instance.'

'What would I know?' He raised his palms to make plain the reasonableness of his position. 'There are a lot of girls up there. Some pretty wild. Girls these days!'

The artist as shocked landlord. Hagen's brows drew down menacingly. Before he could speak, Birge said, 'He was not out in the main part of the hall, or in anybody's doorway or anybody's apartment. His body was to the left of that stairway. He had turned to the left.' The last part was not necessarily true—he could have been attacked on the stairway, staggered up and fallen; he could have been attacked almost anywhere close by and then staggered or fallen to the left of that stairway. But interrogation was almost always like a poker game—bids and bluffs to confuse and draw out the opponent and make him reveal prematurely what he had. Birge laid down another card. 'There are only two apartments to the left. Yours and Miss De Plaissy's.'

Brodovic was silent. Birge yawned, and stretched his arms. 'You said you were in the restaurant all or most of the night. Was Miss De Plaissy?'

The other remained silent a moment longer, then slowly shook his head.

'Well, I don't want to intrude on your private business, Mr. Brodovic. But I think it's time you told us about your relationship with Miss De Plaissy.'

Another long pause. 'You need this?'

'Yes. I think so.' Murder gave him the liberty to ask almost any question not covered by the right against self-incrimination, but he felt a little uncomfortable. Hagen, glaring down, obviously did not.

'Well . . . we live together.'

'You have separate apartments.'

'Well . . . we have each a career. Our own lives. And . . . separated for a while.'

'Then you're not living together now?'

'We see each other all the time.'

'You were never formally married?'

The palms came up again. 'It was the same thing. A long time.'

'How long?'

'Eleven—twelve—years. How many marriages last that long?'

'Being legal makes a difference. For us. I'm not talking about morals.'

Brodovic shrugged. He seemed suddenly bored with the conversation. It did not menace him or praise him. But, after a moment, when Birge did not go on, he looked

59

up, a little warily.

'You say you're separated now, but you still see each other. How close are you?'

'We are not angry. We work together,' he explained in a sort of elliptical way. They had a professional relationship. They pursued art together—he the fine arts, she the commercial. She did not, or could not, handle the great subjects or techniques, but she had a certain facility with water-colors, with designs for decorations for sheets and towels. They had some students. When he had first met her she was earning money hand-painting ties . . . He smiled as though he and Birge had shared a joke. Of course, he said kindly, she was only a girl . . .

Hagen walked restlessly again, then sat down wearily. He was not happy, Birge knew. But he would have to defer to his boss, and let him go his own way. At least for a time.

'I understand. You work together sometimes and are thrown together. But mostly each lives his or her own life.'

'Yes. Yes, of course. Then I'm up much later, in the restaurant, while she sleeps. Then *she's* up, while I sleep. Then she has classes, her own. Like that.'

Birge nodded, in full understanding. He moved a paper before him as though consulting it. He said mildly, 'Then you

60

wouldn't care, or be surprised, if she took another lover?'

Now the face showed real shock. Birge wondered whether it was the idea itself, or its bald and open expression, that had brought on that reaction.

'No! How can a man say such a thing? Now you listen—wait a minute—'

'Wesley Gowen must have been on his way up to see her.' The poker player again, though this time he might be pushing his luck too far. 'Now, what would you do to him—a kid like that—if you caught them together?'

The man rose from his seat. His cheeks were creased and white teeth flashed under the mustache. Birge watched him dispassionately, lifting a couple of fingers to warn Hagen off when it looked as if he might interfere... If this were feigned rage it was beautifully done.

'This is America! What right you have to do this!'

'We're investigating a murder, Mr. Brodovic. All right, please sit down. You are a rather excitable man. I can't blame you this time. But if you've ever been violent, we'll find a record in our files.' He had already checked the files and the computer—one complaint from a man thrown out of the restaurant, which was withdrawn by the man

61

himself when investigation showed that he had been drunk and abusive—but Brodovic might start to worry about what else the police might know.

'She would never! There was nothing, believe me!'

'All right.' He once more moved his papers around.

Brodovic sat, waiting. Birge said, after a pause, 'Well, that's it for now. You can go.'

Hagen, who had just flipped the cigarette butt out the window, turned and stared at Birge. The breeze, coming by him when he had opened the window wider, stirred the blue smoke and diluted it with a sun-warmed freshness. Brodovic also stared a moment, but when the message got through he nodded quickly, got up, and almost ran toward the door.

'We'll be in touch with you,' Birge said. He put out Brodovic's cigarette, left burning on the edge of the ashtray, and looked at the make curiously—not Hagen's standard, unfiltered brand. A foreign make.

'Let it settle a while, Charley. Now, would you ask the woman to come in?'

Hagen turned abruptly, yanked the door open, and muttered something savage to the sergeant outside . . . Fatigue made everyone short-tempered, and Hagen, on this case, had a head start. Still, fatigue to loss of control was, in locker-room scuttlebutt, often ascribed to age and the need to retire. Hagen himself, he understood, had said so . . .

'Charley—don't you think you better get a few hours' sleep now?'

Hagen turned. He let out a slow breath. In a normal voice, hoarsened only by that increasingly sore throat, he said, 'Just through these investigations. Save a briefing.'

Birge hadn't intended rubbing it in; he wanted no enemies on his own staff. But he couldn't be really sorry that Hagen had gotten the message.

CHAPTER FOUR

But when Jeanne De Plaissy came in, Birge suddenly wished that he had ordered Hagen home. The rough approach had been useful with Brodovic; it would probably be harmful now.

He had thought of her, perhaps because of her straight carriage, as a tall woman. She was just as erect, but framed in that doorway in ballet slippers and a thin blouselike gray coat, she no longer seemed as tall. (Was there something about this room—police rooms—

63

that automatically shriveled civilians who came in to be examined? The chief might like it that way, but Birge made a mental note to request a repainting and a revarnishing in a human color.)

He said, 'Come in, Miss De Plaissy, and sit down. Sorry to have kept you waiting so long.' (Despite appearances, this is not Gestapo headquarters!)

Her hair was dark brown, parted in the center, swept smoothly to and bound in the back—thick, hardly a wave—leaving the brow high and clear. The eyes, as he remembered, were steady. She came, without a word, and sat down. She wore no makeup and he could see that she hadn't slept. She unbuttoned the top buttons of the coat. The dress under it was black. She waited, with blank, but not dead, eyes.

He started to say that he was sorry that they should meet under such circumstances—and stopped himself in time. The standard undertaker's line. Undertakers and homicide detectives had too many things in common.

'You seem to have known Wesley Gowen quite well. Just tell me about it.'

She took a moment to answer—as though quietly thinking about it. 'Does it make much difference now?'

'We have to investigate, Miss De Plaissy.'

'It can't have had much to do with his death.'

Birge sighed. 'You may know that, but we have to find out. We won't keep probing into any personal area that isn't relevant to what we have to investigate... Just go ahead. I'll stop you if it gets too far out.'

Another pause. She had high cheekbones, and, this close, it seemed to Birge that the skin was drawn tightly over them, making those areas pale and hollowing the cheeks. But she did not clasp her hands or show other signs of nervousness. 'He was very young.'

He waited. When she did not go on he said, 'He was twenty-one.'

'Oh ... isn't that young?'

'Miss De Plaissy, what does that mean? He was an adult.'

'He was quite young. That's what I remember most about him. He was at the age when he would sit there—I guess you could say that his eyes were shining.'

Birge waited.

'Well you asked about our ... relationship. He was so ... eager to know. I guess that's what ... attracted me.' For the first time she made a little gesture with one hand, then let it fall.

'And?'

'Nothing. We had this little group, you see.

65

Used to gather sometimes in my apartment, often quite late. Well, it wasn't exactly a class; some young people from my classes—I used to teach a little art, you know, or design—would come too, but I wouldn't charge. I don't know how he got in, exactly. He didn't really belong. He would come and sit quietly in the restaurant, and after a while he ... sort of came up with the group.'

'I don't quite understand. How did you meet him?'

'Well ... nothing really definite. He would come in occasionally, I guess after work. After midnight—or one o'clock—on weeknights, people often come in who are just lonely. Or bored. They sometimes come in alone. Mirko never turns anybody away as long as they keep buying, even women alone. Most are men. I remember when Wesley first came in. He sort of looked around as though to see if the place were real. Then sat down as though waiting.'

'For what?'

'I don't know. Something.'

'So?'

She sighed. 'Well, then ... he started to talk to people. Some people. Some of the people who come there, you know—they have different theories about art or mankind or ... whatever. He would listen, sometimes discuss their ideas with them. That was all some

66

needed. You know—there are people who worry about the environment, or who eat only certain kinds of foods. I don't mean by that that they are crazy people or anything like that. Some think they're artists. Or that they can influence politics.'

'All right.'

'I mean, he listened, even if it was ridiculous. He never made fun of anybody.'

'Did he always come in alone?'

'No. He brought girls a couple of times. Those were earlier in the evening. I guess he was off work those evenings, and wanted to show the place to others. And once he came in with another man, later; I guess someone from work. The man didn't seem interested. Kept shaking his head. He made suggestive remarks to me. I thought we might have to throw him out. But he didn't find what he wanted, so he left early. None of those he brought ever came back. At least not while I was in the restaurant. Only Wesley. I don't come in every night, and I don't stay late, usually.'

The poker player put down a card to liven the game. 'How did you get to know him so well?'

'I didn't know him very well, really. I don't think anyone did.'

Birge frowned. 'Miss De Plaissy, we're not

getting very far, are we?'

'Well, I'm answering all your questions, sir.'

Birge tapped his pencil. 'You knew him quite well. You say you saw him frequently in the restaurant. You sat with him and talked with him, didn't you? . . . All right, you took part in discussions when he was there. And then he was invited—or came along up to—your apartment.'

'Yes.'

'Were you alone together much?'

'Well, later on—recently—he would sometimes come up. To talk. Mostly in the day . . . It was not like—I think you mean. While I work, sometimes people stop in. I can talk—or at least listen—while I'm drawing or painting. Especially when it's routine work. Flowers for silkscreen—that sort of thing. Friends might drop in.'

He was sure that Hagen's eyes, under gathered brows, were on her; he was sure that they were saying that the police were seeking to find the motive for a murder, not this chitchat. Birge was careful not to look at him or to give him an opening to intrude with his questions, because she was probably not merely chatting but burying the questions to avoid the answers—and, probably, the memories.

68

'Friends might drop in,' Birge repeated.

She could have just let it lie there, not answer, and wait. But she seemed to be as afraid of accumulated silence as of frankness. 'Yes. Many people—of those I meet—want to talk. Not just chat, but want to have somebody listen to them. In the city, you know, most people won't listen. And somebody who stays busy with something else, his own form of expression—and seems to be pleasant, and I guess receptive—and doesn't *judge* ... It *is* remarkable how popular that person can be.' At the end the note changed.

'What did Wesley Gowen talk about?'

'At first, not much. If anybody else stopped in he'd just listen. He asked questions. My life, the people there. You know.'

'Afraid I don't.'

'He was such a *boy* ... Later he said that he asked and listened because he wanted to find out about things. Life. What people did. Said he wanted to be a writer.' She released her breath. It was not quite a sigh. Birge automatically followed her eyes to the ceiling; he saw nothing but familiar stains from an old leak.

'Many writers?'

'Many ... they want to write at least one book, I think. Everybody has a story or a long

69

complaint.'

Once more the business of shifting the papers on his desk—like cards. 'But he didn't. Just wanted to find out about things.'

'Well, recently he started to talk a little about his own problems. Not much chance to do what he wanted to do. Having to work at that place when he wanted to ... well, do other things. Get experiences. Be a writer.' For the first time she smiled, a small smile. 'Afraid I didn't pay much attention. They all say something like that, sooner or later. And he hardly talked at all when others were there. I don't think he mentioned it more than once or twice.' That smile again—this time a little more apologetic. 'Everybody else's problems always seem so small. And sometimes ... well, you know.'

'But when you two were alone together, he was more relaxed. Talked more.'

'Oh yes.'

'And recently you've been alone together more often. More time.'

She was silent. Her profile was toward Birge; her hands lay loosely on her lap. Nothing visible to him moved.

'Miss De Plaissy, Mr. Brodovic tells me that you and he lived together—in effect like man and wife—for a number of years. Is that right?'

She remained silent. He said, 'Understand, we have no desire to pry into your personal affairs. But we have to know a little more about the circumstances surrounding Mr. Gowen's death.'

'Mirko said that?'

'I don't remember the exact words. But to that effect.'

'How would any of that help you investigate . . . the death?'

'We want to find out. I can assure you that we don't want to discuss anything we find not related to Mr. Gowen.' His pad, on which he had taken notes during the Brodovic interview—and on which he had been doodling during this one—was close to his right hand. He moved it in front of him.

'Now. You've said that you would see Wesley Gowen fairly frequently, sometimes in the restaurant, and quite often in your apartment. Sometimes in your apartment during the day—presumably before he went to work, or on days off—but sometimes also at night. Sometimes as part of a group, that little group that would come to your apartment occasionally to talk . . . about art, problems, the environment, and so on—and sometimes alone. When the two of you were alone, he was more frank, more confiding. He apparently felt he had found someone he

71

could confide in and trust—sympathetic, warm—he must have felt that. You indicate that he was quite young—"such a boy." Quite lonely. You are an attractive woman. You say that as time went on, these sessions, when you were alone together, grew more frequent.' Birge lifted and turned the top sheet on his pad, as though he had been writing on it and had reached the bottom.

She shook her head as though she couldn't believe what she was hearing. 'But that . . . but it didn't mean . . .'

'I think that's what you told me. If I got any of it wrong, please help me straighten it out.'

'But it wasn't the way you . . . make it sound! It's—it was—all so harmless! What a mind you have! We just talked. He was just a boy who wanted to talk!'

Birge smiled slightly. He nodded gravely, as though chewing on that thought. 'On the other hand . . . is that the way it seemed to him?'

She kept shaking her head.

'And is that the way it seemed to Brodovic?'

She turned sharply. 'Why, he knew about this all the time. It's something we've discussed. More than once. To some extent— well, we both do a little teaching. And talking to our students. What did he say about it?'

'I don't remember that he mentioned it

specifically. But I also don't get the impression that he is aware of ... private conversations like those you describe.'

'Are you implying something, sir?'

'Just repeating what you said. I believe you. And, as *you* imply, it's none of my business. What might be my business is how Brodovic sees it, how *he* might react. I get the impression—correct me if I'm wrong—that he might on occasion be a violent man.' Brodovic hadn't, finally, been very aggressive in this office moments ago, but it had not escaped Birge over the years that many men with fearsome reputations, particularly when home with their women, were quite well behaved in the homicide office. He caught Hagen's eye; Charley was relaxed, for a change, almost smiling.

But her reaction was not what he had expected. She was not upset; she made no denials. She seemed to grow very calm. Her hands smoothed the folds of her coat on her lap. She said, 'That's ridiculous.'

'You mean it's not true?'

A wave of her hand dismissed the whole subject. 'It's ridiculous because what I do is none of his business.'

'Oh? Does he understand that?'

'We don't even have to discuss it. What you didn't mention—or he didn't bother to tell

73

you—is that though we did live together for years—almost man and wife as you say—we've lived apart for about as many years. I wonder why he didn't mention that?'

'What you're saying now is that he knows he has no claim on you and wouldn't do anything about your association with anyone else?'

'That's right.'

But men don't always act the way they should. Particularly men who worry about their manhood, and humiliation. 'Well, I hope you're sure.'

Her face—that remarkable self-possession—suddenly seemed to crack. 'Why do we have to talk about this!'

'Beg pardon?'

'He was just a boy! Why can't everybody understand that? In a way a foolish boy... Why do you insist I have to be involved with him? Am I a young girl? Is that the way he should be remembered?'

She had a point. To the homicide division Gowen existed as a victim whose history would be important only if it helped lead them to a criminal ... You are correct, Miss De Plaissy—the dead probably deserve better. On the other hand, Miss De Plaissy, aren't you being a touch too innocent? You know that you are an attractive woman no more than

74

thirty—and you know what I'm getting at . . .

'The fact that he was young, and maybe as nice as you describe him, would make it important that we find out why he was killed, I think . . . Sorry, I didn't want to lecture.' Time to soften up . . . After a time, as Collender had once said about *his* work, everything becomes technique. She might confide soon, he thought tiredly, if I now take it easy.

But Hagen said in that hoarse voice, 'Brodovic—was he the guy who did the bouncing?'—and the tone stiffened her.

'What?'

'You said—the man who came in with Gowen—that he got obnoxious and somebody was going to throw him out. Who did the bouncing? Brodovic?'

'Well, we both—or even Ginnie, the waitress—we'd warn people, or tell them to leave. That's usually—almost always—enough.'

'But Brodovic did throw some out. We know it. In that neighborhood you have to be pretty tough, or at least loud.'

'I don't know about that. We don't have those kinds of customers.'

We, Birge thought.

'You've seen him slap people around,' Hagen croaked. 'You know about it.'

75

'Let's pin a few points down,' Birge said. 'Did you see Wesley Gowen in your apartment last night? Or after midnight?'

She shook her head vigorously.

'Anyplace upstairs?'

'No.'

Maybe it had not been too bright a question. It seemed pretty clear, from the way the body lay, that Gowen had probably been facing forward, and therefore most probably had just come up the steps, just starting to turn, not going the other way.

Still—'on the other hand'!—he could have been called and turned to face someone. And since he hadn't thrown up that arm or taken any discernible action to protect himself, it would have been someone he trusted, or at least didn't know he had much reason to mistrust.

And on that third hand that Hagen had mentioned, had Gowen been fully and consciously facing someone, he would have seen the weapon and received some warning . . .

'Earlier in the evening? Downstairs? Anywhere?'

He noted, both mentally and on his pad, the half second she took this time before her no.

'Well, we won't pursue it further now. Thank you, Miss De Plaissy. You aren't

76

leaving on a trip or anything like that, are you?'

'No.'

'All right ... oh, by the way...' A face floated into his memory. 'Do you have a child?'

'Yes.'

'Sex and age?'

'He's a boy. Almost twelve.'

'Does he stay in his father's apartment?'

'Where?'

'That front apartment—directly over the restaurant—isn't that Mr. Brodovic's?'

'Mirko is not his father.'

'All right, thank you again. We'll be in touch very soon.'

Hagen rolled from his half-seat on the sill over to the door and opened it for her. Then they all sat for a moment, still as in a tableau, before she turned her head and said, 'Then I'm free to go?'

Birge nodded. She returned the nod, as though part of a politeness ceremony, and rose. As she approached the door she moved to the side, apparently as far as she could get from Hagen, before passing through. Birge noted that it seemed to be the first time she showed anything resembling fear. But she nodded to Hagen too—so it probably wasn't fear.

'Maybe I had better go home,' Hagen said. 'I'm beginning to turn off the customers.'

Birge agreed.

CHAPTER FIVE

But after Hagen had retrieved his hat, tipped it at him, and started through the door after the woman, Birge suddenly remembered something and changed his mind. 'Just one more, Charley. You might want to see this one. Send in the young fellow out there, the last one.'

He was not a particularly impressive young man—about five-nine, sandy straight hair with the front trailing down over his left forehead except when shoved back with an abrupt upward thrust with his left hand. He wore the uniform blue jeans, somewhat worn, though clean and whole, but above that, surprisingly, a sport jacket, light blue shirt, dark tie. Birge suspected that was put on for the occasion. He was also cleanly shaven, which he hadn't been near dawn this morning. Altogether he looked a good deal like dozens of others who might pass unnoticed on the state university campus, which was not famous either for the hippie mode or the suited business school students. He might be a little older than most—about twenty-five—but he could certainly blend without notice in the groups that crowded out of the buses for the evening classes and surged across Broad St. as the lights changed.

Hagen was right behind, eyebrows raised that familiar quarter of an inch. Birge signaled to his lieutenant to close the door firmly, then motioned the young man to the chair alongside the desk.

Hagen took his half-seat on the sill. Birge looked down at his desk once more as though consulting one of the scattered sheets. 'You're ... Ralph Hutkin.' He looked up. 'Did I pronounce that right?'

'Yes sir.' His voice was a little flat and slightly slurred, as all young voices seemed these days, but still rather pleasant. This close, Birge could see that, under a fading tan, he was light-complexioned with a few freckles across the straight nose. The all-American boy from the *SatEve-Post* covers—that only older people seemed to remember well.

Birge leaned back, still examining him, no longer bothering to look at his desk top. 'Probationary Patrolman Ralph Hutkin, that is.'

He could hear Hagen's feet come down hard on the floor. Without turning his head

79

Birge said, 'Sorry, Charley. Couldn't mention it before. We were always with third parties.' He nodded toward Hutkin. 'I recognized him from classes in the academy.' For years he had watched such ordinary, bland but distinct faces, like those of boys just off the corners, facing him in the rows of classes in the police academy, just starting to become uniform through the identical short haircuts, then moving to the identical, badly fitting uniforms that would grow to them like their skins so that eventually even when the uniforms were off, it was as though they still wore the badge labeled 'cop'... The process had hardly started with this boy, so not even Hagen could tell.

Birge said to Hutkin, 'You on the late shift, so you can afford to hang around that late in a place like that?'

'Yes sir. For this week. But today happens to be my day off too.'

'You're not on special assignment of any kind? You shouldn't be while still a probationary, unless for very special circumstances.'

'No sir.'

'Well ... we can't, and I wouldn't want to, tell you where you can spend your leisure time. With certain obvious exceptions, of course, and you were told all about those in

80

the academy. Still, even in places where there's no question of possible law violation as far as we know, you're expected to use some sense. Yes, I know you're likely to see old-time cops almost anywhere, but *you're* still on probation. All right ... what were you doing there?'

'Well sir, it's my evening—night off, and I just thought I'd go somewhere. No particular reason.'

'I didn't see any girl with you. Were you alone?'

'I came alone, sir.'

'Hutkin, as you know—or you'd better learn—when a murder has been committed, practically no one—and especially a police officer—who happens to be on the scene has much right to privacy. What really brought you there?'

He seemed a little confused by the questioning—and apprehensive because of Birge's tone and rank. 'No particular reason. I had no date. I ran across the place some time ago and thought it might be interesting.'

'Then you've been there before. How often?'

'Two, three times. Not often. It's not my favorite place or anything like that, sir.'

'You ever been there with a date? Or talked much about yourself? I mean, is there anybody connected with that place, or who might walk in, who knows who you are?'

'I don't see how, sir. They wouldn't know I was a police officer anyhow.'

'You mean you never talked about this place with anybody from your old neighborhood or your class or anything like that?'

'No sir.'

Birge recalled very briefly De Plaissy's story about Wesley Gowen's friend or coworker who apparently simply couldn't understand why anybody would go there, made himself obnoxious with the women, and left early. Hutkin, older and with a little police savvy, could probably anticipate better how his acquaintances would react and be trusted not to tell them . . . But why was he so different from them? What really attracted him? And how did this—orientation?—fit in with what the chief, and others, looked for in accepting applicants—their 'desirable police profile'?

'How well did you know Wesley Gowen?'

'Not at all, sir.'

'Not at all? You mean you never even saw him there? In a place that small you didn't notice him, or talk to him?'

'No sir. Never talked to him, or even noticed him. If he was there anytime I was I didn't observe him. And I believe—I'm sure—I would have.'

He was 'sure'... Birge pushed back from his desk. 'When did you come in?'

'About midnight, I think, sir.'

'Mr. Hutkin, you're here on official police business, and I can have you suspended and possibly discharged for lying to me!'

'But captain, sir—'

'You came in about midnight and stayed there and you didn't see him come in at all?'

'No sir! Except maybe for the couple of times I was in the men's room. I drank beer, sir—'

'Then where was he before he went upstairs?'

'I don't know, sir. He must have gone straight upstairs. I hadn't been to the men's room just before then. I was getting ready to go home. Nothing happening.'

Birge paused a moment. Straight upstairs? An appointment—not a conversation in the restaurant leading to a casual invitation?

In a more relaxed tone he said, 'What do you mean by "nothing happening"? What were you hoping would happen?'

'Nothing really, sir.'

'Hutkin, were you trying to promote that waitress?' The youth started to turn red— perhaps from being challenged this way rather than from being 'found out.' 'All right, son, your business is yours. Although the police department expects you to use some discretion ... And if you don't, I guess the thing to do is to plan not to be there during a murder investigation.'

Once more he lapsed into silence. Then: 'Hutkin, how well did you know those two out there? What about Brodovic?'

'Well, he's the proprietor, sir.'

'I'm aware of that!'

'I mean—he just says hello, do you like it here, will you have anything else to drink? He watches you to see that you keep spending. But I don't know him personally. Not really to talk to.'

'And the woman, Miss De Plaissy?'

He was a little more guarded now. 'She's not always there, sir ... Yes sir, I *am* answering ... Well, sometimes she comes in and sits down with guests. She's very popular, I think—that is, lots of those people are her friends or something. I think she has classes upstairs. She likes to make them welcome. So, since I've been coming in alone, she sits with me sometimes.'

So that's why you go there, Birge thought. At least that's why you came back. The friendly lady. 'She sat down with Wesley Gowen too. Are you certain now you didn't see him there, in the group?'

84

'Well, you can't judge anybody very clearly on the floor like that.' He stopped, frowning in concentration—and probably also remembering that Birge would know a great deal more about the subject than he. 'Couldn't see him so clear . . . but no sir, I'm sure.'

'Well, you weren't there very often, you say . . . All right. Are you a member of a class there, or a group? Did you ever go upstairs to her apartment or Brodovic's?'

'No, sir. I've just been a customer.'

Birge motioned to Hagen, who came over. 'Hutkin, I'm going to put you on special assignment . . . Yes, I know I'm not your chief, but I'll fix it up with him. You'll start tomorrow. You can report to me or to Lt. Hagen, whomever is here, every couple of days or whenever you find something interesting. It won't be hard work. I just want you to go to that place—go there every night unless it gets suspicious—or as often as you can—and hang around until you become a member of a class, or the group that meets with De Plaissy. Stick your nose in everything. You're a searcher after beauty or something.' Hagen snorted. 'Or, like the Gowen boy, you're bored with your job and you're sensitive, and you want a little—I guess it's "life." As soon as you can, bring up Gowen. That won't seem forced. You were

85

there, you would be concerned—so would they—you would naturally worry and ask—it could be a way to get in, to get De Plaissy interested in you—and Brodovic, if he's interested in anything besides himself.'

Birge raised his arms in a seventh-inning stretch, yawned, and rubbed the back of his neck. 'Remember, you're on duty. I want all the information I can pick up about Wesley Gowen and their connection with him. And all the circumstances that led to his death. That's all you're going there for, remember.' Birge looked hard at the young face. 'You have *no* other loyalties ... Well, you better report here every afternoon—that assignment won't keep you busy eight hours a day—unless you can expand it. Into the apartments, and so on. Lt. Hagen can fix up your time schedules ... Okay, that's all. Turn up there this evening full of concern and questions. See if you can talk to Brodovic and De Plaissy alone. And ... we don't have very much time.'

The young man nodded. But, like the woman, he didn't seem to know he had been dismissed. Or maybe his precinct captain always made him wait for formal dismissal. 'All right, that's all ... check him out, Charley.'

Hagen motioned his head toward the door. His face showed neither approval nor disapproval. Hutkin rose, and hesitated, still facing Birge, before following Hagen. For a mad moment Birge thought he was about to salute. 'One more thing,' the older man said. 'You see Hagen or myself in there—or any other cop—you're not working for us. Understand?'

'Yes sir.'

'Nobody's there for pleasure. None of *us*, anyway . . . goodbye.'

★   ★   ★

Hutkin and Hagen went to the outer office to arrange details, and then both left—Hagen, presumably, finally to bed. Birge got into his routine paperwork for that day and was getting ready to leave himself—to go out into the last of that sunshine under those maples—when the phone call came and was put through to him, as he had instructed. 'Sam? Sam?'—an insistent question.

'Yes, Haskell. You all finished?'

'Well, tests and analyses—stomach contents for toxic materials and so on—aren't all in yet. We're giving this one special attention, as you wanted. But I did say I'd call if anything unusual came along . . . But I'm not even sure if this is unusual, or what it is. It could even be a mistake or accident.'

87

'What?'

'If it's carelessness, I'm going to ride somebody's back.'

'Get to the point, Haskell.'

'Well, I'm stalling because I don't want to stir up anything because of some attendant's dumb error ... All right. Well, after examining it and photographing it and so on, we cleaned up the main wound, and I had the dried blood—some of it—given routine analysis. Touching all bases. I didn't do it myself—but Joe Castle has about the best pair of eyes on the microscope of anybody here. Anyway, he called me over to show me something funny. A little speck of the clots wouldn't dissolve and wasn't blood. Different shade. We took it to the lab and made sure ... Paint.'

'Paint? You certain?'

'Considering its size, yeah. That's an easy enough test.'

'You didn't notice anything else that might have come with it? Tiny sliver? Metal? Wood splinter?'

'No.'

'What about inside the wound itself?'

'This was inside the wound.'

'Try further analysis. What kind of paint? For wood? Metal? Furniture?'

Collender sounded a little abashed. 'Gone

by this time, Sam. Too small anyway, I think, for that kind of detail.'

Birge swore under his breath. Collender must have heard the mutter. 'I thought you should know, Sam, but I don't think you should get excited. He could have picked it up almost anywhere, even before death, and it could have been hammered in. Anyplace around—bumped into the wall, the floor . . .'

'There was nothing like that on the floor.'

There was a pause. 'I know. That's why I checked. And called.'

CHAPTER SIX

One more stop: that 'small house in Overland Hills.'

Birge resolutely turned his mind away from the sentimental overtones of that designation—like a daytime soap—and heaved himself out of his car, which, he concluded for the thousandth time, had not been built for men his size. He looked up at the house on its high, slightly eroded lawn.

Overland Hills had not prospered; the anticipated large expansion of a nearby auto-assembly plant had run into the recession and not taken place. The disappointment had had some good effects: Since the developer had quickly abandoned his original plans, the houses were not all made from the same cookie cutter. Some older ones had been left as well as many trees, and the buildings and streets had retained some individuality. But there remained vacant lots, occasionally overgrown with weeds, a few unfinished foundations, and some sidewalks that ended abruptly, nowhere. The Gowen block seemed dreary, as in a declining mill town.

Their house was small—probably because Mr. Gowen had had only two sons, who could sleep in a single bedroom, and not much money anyway. The builder had not apparently worried much about the quality of construction; there were cracks in the foundation and in a couple of gray—turning green—asbestos shingles. But the place was neat; the small uphill lawn clipped; and somebody, probably Wesley, had recently started to paint exterior trim and rusty guttering—a downspout was a brilliant white and a paint bucket was under the picture window.

Probably the inside, the mother's domain, would be even neater.

It was on a rise; he climbed two short flights of steps, at right angles, to get to the front door. If somebody—especially somebody old—slipped at the top on an icy morning, it would be too bad.

A small black wreath already on the door. Everything correct.

He caught his breath, then pressed the bell. He wished now he had called first. Experience had taught him that it was usually better just to drop by to try to get information from survivors—to call first was often to invite trouble or argument. But this time—a mother alone—might be the exception ... Perhaps he also should have brought someone—not Hagen—maybe a woman, Judy or even his wife, with him.

A gray-haired woman in black looked down at him through the three angled narrow panes in the upper door, then opened it about three inches. She did not unhook the chain. 'Yes?'

'Mrs. Gowen?'

'What do you want her for?'

'Are you her sister?'

'There's been a death in this house. Would you state your business, please?'

He sighed. In fiction, tragedy was usually so clean, unencumbered by frustrations and embarrassments. 'I'm Captain Birge of the police department. I'm here on official business. Unless Mrs. Gowen is too ill to speak to anybody, would you please let her know I'm here?'

'Well ...' The voice was a little less certain, but the eyes did not become more friendly nor the opening wider. 'I'll have to see. She *is* lying down.'

'Thank you.' Ostentatiously he glanced at his watch.

In a little while he heard voices inside in unclear argument except for the statement by the woman who had answered the door that 'you *must* rest! That comes first!' Then another face appeared in that crack, a shorter woman, hollowed cheeks, large, harassed eyes below gray streaks—with the first woman's scolding face floating just above—and in a few seconds the door was pushed toward closing to allow the chain to be disengaged, and then it was opened.

'Yes?' Mrs. Gowen said. 'What was it you said you wanted?'

'I'm Captain Birge from police headquarters. I'm investigating the death of your son.' He did not say more, but stared meaningfully past them—they still blocked the doorway—into the house. He did not want to discuss these matters while standing, nor outside, nor in front of the other woman.

Mrs. Gowen nodded slowly, as though considering the thought, and stepped aside. The other woman had to step back too. 'All right. Please come in.'

'Thank you.'

She kept nodding, but now toward the open doorway to the living room, to his left just off the tiny hall. She walked ahead, a small black figure, bent forward slightly and limping a little on her left leg. He followed. The other woman, hovering around Birge's shoulder as though trying to get past him to Mrs. Gowen, brought up the rear.

'This is Mrs. McCluskey,' the mother said. 'A dear neighbor, who kindly came over to help.' Birge nodded. The other woman barely responded.

The gray-and-red carpet had worn spots before the chairs and the TV table, but was otherwise scrupulously clean. He could not tell the condition of the furniture because of the carefully fitted coverings. A family photograph—man, woman, two small boys— had the place of honor on the wall over the sofa. Next to the picture window, which he faced, Jesus, in white and in gentle Nordic profile, gazed sadly upward to the ceiling.

'May I get Wesley now?'

'Probably not quite yet. I can check. But if you'll give me the name of your undertaker I can make the arrangements for you.' Not his job, but it seemed little enough. He also knew that if he talked to that undertaker he could keep the fee down, and that too seemed little enough.

She did not argue. 'I can see him soon?'

'I can arrange it. But it might be better to contact the undertaker first.'

'I . . . don't really have an undertaker.'

'I can recommend one, Mattie,' Mrs. McCluskey said quickly. 'A very good one. He's taken care of all our funerals. So sympathetic. And reasonable.'

'Let's sit down,' Birge said.

'You take the easy chair, dear,' Mrs. McCluskey said. 'And put your feet on the hassock. You must not agitate yourself.' For an instant Birge was confused as to whose house it was.

He said, 'I think we had better hold this interview in private, Mrs. Gowen. Personal matters.' Mrs. McCluskey's mouth and eyes formed O's. Damn it, why was he bothering to explain? He added, 'And confidential police business. Please!'

Mrs. Gowen said serenely, 'It's all right, sir. Jenny will understand.'

Mrs. McCluskey looked as though she were about to complain. But Mrs. Gowen had sat on the chair she had designated and perhaps that reassured her. She lifted the other woman's feet onto the hassock, told her to be sure to stop if the questioning became a strain, glared once at Birge, and left—to where, Birge

94

was sure, she could stand just outside the door and listen.

Her departure seemed to allow Mrs. Gowen to relax. She raised her hand to shade her eyes and sat that way quietly for a moment, head bowed. Birge waited. She then inhaled, straightened somewhat, and raised a lace-trimmed handkerchief to her nose.

'We are ... extremely sorry that this has happened. And that I have to question you like this.'

She nodded. 'That's all right.' Her voice had grown soft and hoarse.

'I think you know the circumstances of your son's death.' It suddenly struck him as strange, and negligent, that she hadn't been taken down earlier to positively identify the body. He had left it to Hagen, and Hagen must have been too tired—especially since, for his purposes, they already had positive identification. Probably Judy, being a woman before being an officer, had decided it shouldn't be done at that time. She had shown photographs—probably choosing the least shocking—and that must have been enough. Still, it seemed unusual that Mrs. Gowen hadn't herself insisted, to remove all doubt, on the hopeless chance that maybe ... and simply to see ...

'I didn't want to repeat what you already

95

know, from the policewoman's visit.'

She nodded again.

'Did you know that place where he ... died? That apartment building? Or the stores or that restaurant, Petit Montmartre, under it?'

'No I'm sorry. He never took me there.'

'Well, no reason why you should. Then he never talked about it with you?'

'No.'

'And he never discussed any friends he had there? Or any that he might have taken there?'

'Well, he sometimes talked about stopping to have coffee, or visit someplace on the way home, when I asked him about getting more sleep to keep up his strength. And, you know, I knew of course that he was studying to be a writer, and sometimes he said he had to gather material. I knew about that.'

'Then he did want to be a writer?'

'Oh yes. He even attended classes when he could. At the university campus branch close to ... to that place.' Now the reserve broke; the chin trembled and she brought the handkerchief up to it and held it there for a while as they both sat silently. Then when she spoke, her voice was higher and hesitant, each word like an uncertain step on an unstable ledge. 'He wanted to. But he had to work. To support me ... our house.'

'Then in general you don't know the places he went to after work. Besides school. I mean—did he sometimes work an earlier shift that let him go to school after work?'

'Not this semester. No, I didn't want to check on him. Anything like that. A boy like that . . . has to have some freedom.'

'Well, that's very understanding. Did you know his friends?'

'He brought some boys home for dinner. They were rather rough . . . I don't think they were really friends. Just boys from work. I think he was trying to make friends.' She stirred, raised the handkerchief again.

'What about girls?'

She looked at him. 'I wanted him to meet girls. Asked him to attend church. I even called the youth club of the nearest church— Overland Hills Presbyterian, I think you can see the steeple maybe out that window—but he didn't want to go.' Her eyes stayed on him . . . But did she really want to know? 'He didn't have a girl . . . to go with regularly.'

He nodded, this time encouragingly.

'I don't mean he didn't date girls. Once in a while. There was a girl he met in class. He told me about her. But not, maybe, more than once. He was kind of shy. He never brought one home . . . I know he would have talked to me about anything serious.'

97

'Yes.' He seemed to have gotten about as much information as he could by questioning, at least at this time. 'I guess there's not much point in asking if you know whether he had any enemies?'

'No. Oh no.' She breathed a little faster for a moment, seemed restless. 'None that I knew about . . . I can only tell you what I know about.'

'Well, Mrs. Gowen, for me to have come now was, I know, a terrible burden for you. I'll keep quiet now, and you might just want to talk about Wesley.'

'Anything?'

'Anything you might want to say. I'd just like to know him better.' He had wanted to add 'and you too,' but decided at the last instant to leave that out. 'That is, if it's not too much of a strain.'

'No. Not at all.' Some color came back to her face. Conversation brought life. 'I'd like to.' She got up from the chair and moved toward the sofa—he thought toward him, but she leaned past him and pointed to the picture on the wall. 'That's him. The small boy.'

Birge rose and dutifully looked where she pointed—an old family portrait, carefully posed in the studio of a neighborhood photographer—father stiff, small mother carefully smiling, her hand on the shoulder of

98

the taller boy, who looked as though he had been called just as the shutter snapped, so that his face, starting to grin, was turned away and slightly blurred. The finger of the live mother was pointing at the smaller boy, who stared straight at the camera, literally following the instructions to be absolutely still. He was not an unusual-looking child. Birge noted that the mother seemed to be leaning a little to one side. Probably her limp was an old one.

'Very handsome boy.' Actually there seemed no indication of the talent or uniqueness the mother described; he could not have been distinguished in a crowd.

'Yes, isn't he?' As if he were still alive. For that matter as if that family still existed . . . She kept smiling at it. Then: 'This is my other son, John. John Wesley Gowen. He's out West. Doing very well. I hope he can manage to be here for the funeral.'

Birge nodded. Undoubtedly she had that hope.

Her vague, dark eyes turned to him. 'Would you like to see his room?'

He had been wondering how he could decently ask to see her son's papers and effects, to see what mention he might find of others, especially De Plaissy, and of habits and associations that the mother did not know about. Now she was offering them to him—

99

because she had become convinced that he was a nice man, sincerely interested in her nice boy. 'Yes I would,' he said. 'Thank you very much.'

'Well, just follow me.' She smiled, probably more to herself than to him, and turned.

He noted the limp again. 'Shouldn't you have a cane? Or something like that?'

'Oh, I never use it in the house.' She motioned him to follow and went on ahead—not, he noted thankfully, toward the door behind which Mrs. McCluskey was undoubtedly hiding.

He was afraid that he would have to watch her climb steps ahead of him, but the upstairs was apparently an attic or some kind of spare bedroom; the bedrooms in use, though small, were all on this floor, perhaps to save her that climb. She went through a small dining room (lilies, with a card, in the center of the table), past a bathroom, and into a bedroom with windows that looked into the backyard and, to the right, onto a walkway between their house and the next. On the wall was a high school banner and on top of the bookcases a football painted white, losing its air. He suspected that they were from the older son—no particular reason, except that some of the other items on display were obviously his: picture postcards from Germany, a framed snapshot of a soldier.

But in the corner was a card table with a portable typewriter in its closed—and probably dusted—case, and next to it a file folder with paper inside, all held down by a paperweight. Under the table—to the right, where it would not interfere with the feet of the typist but was handy for him—was a cardboard box, its top carefully cut to convert it into a file. In it were more folders with visible papers, some closed manila envelopes, and a few magazines—on the spine of one he saw the title *Writer's World*.

'This is Wesley,' she said. He turned. She was pointing to a face in one of two framed pictures of high school graduating classes, the boys in identical black mortarboards and gowns, the girls in identical white. The face her finger touched, like the young child's face in the family portrait, gazed straight and unsmiling into the eyes of the viewer.

'Did he stay alone here most of the time?'

'This was his and John's room, and when John was home of course he stayed here too. They got along very well. I remember John kidding Wesley about the papers he left around, the stories. He liked to kid... But John was in the army a long time, and of course he's been out West, earning his living for the past few years. Wesley didn't mind being alone. I could hear his typewriter going sometimes, and I didn't want to interfere. Except, of course, to bring in clean linen and clothes and to clean up. But I usually waited until he was gone at work for that.' And then to the anticipated question—which Birge had not thought to ask—'I never wanted to intrude. I never looked at his papers unless he asked me to. I did come in sometimes to tell him that he needed more sleep and should rest more, or what did he want for supper—things like that.'

How could he ask her for permission—or to leave—so that he could search the place? A boy who fancied himself a writer ought to keep some kind of notebook, diary, address book. A lot of junk to wade through, but it might possibly include something of the friends and experiences he had had, and names perhaps. Thoughts, feelings. An interview beyond the grave—in this case, beyond Haskell's morgue.

'I kept his things neat for him. He sometimes got to thinking so much that he didn't clean up. You know how boys are.' She pulled out the relatively thin top drawer of the chest of drawers—the one in which, in Birge's own house, Roy used to put tie clips, cuff links, and snapshots of old girlfriends. In this one, in addition to similar items, he saw, carefully arranged, several knives. One was a

Boy Scout knife in its case, but another was an illegal switch-blade. 'It was a hobby he had when he was a teenager,' she said. 'He hasn't collected any lately. But he used to enjoy it so much.'

Idly, Birge lifted the paperweight—a chipped metal dog with floppy ears—and riffled through the edges of the sheets. Mostly they were roughly typed, with many pencil corrections, but about halfway down were two pictures, cut from magazines, of female nudes. He closed it quickly and put back the paperweight. She was at his elbow now, watching what he was doing—but he did not believe she had seen the photos.

'I never really looked through his things,' she said. 'But I suppose it's all right now.' She looked up into Birge's eyes for some kind of affirmation. 'He had a lot of talent. Sometimes he read me things. Here, I'll show you.'

He expected her to draw something from the box underneath. Instead she held a tall, rather thin book with an embossed cover the general color of foil. She waited until he had digested that cover—the silver anniversary edition of the yearbook of Omar Nelson Bradley High School—and opened it to a page marked by a ribbon: 'Poetical Lament' by Wesley A. Gowen.

Oh, Inspiration, hear me plead!
Help me in my hour of need!

It continued on for six full stanzas.

He said, 'It's very nice.'

She said, 'I know you think it's just high school. But his English teacher said he had talent!' She began to tremble, and put her hand on the card table to steady herself. Under the weight it trembled too.

Birge took her arm. His fist seemed to go all around it. 'Here, you'd better sit down.'

'No, no.'

But she let him lead her to the nearest chair, against the side window—apparently the same chair Wesley had used when typing—and she sat. 'He often asked my advice. I said I would learn to type, and help, but he said ... He read me one story about a mother. Her boy went off to the army, and he never came back, and she thought he was dead ... but he was just off working somewhere ... It was so sweet. It was one of those he sent out.'

'I think I've tired you out too much. Perhaps I'd better leave. I'll call Mrs.—uh— McCluskey.' He was surprised that the other woman had not rushed in already.

Mrs. Gowen took his hand, first in one and then in both of hers. She raised her head and stared intently at him. One of the wings of her parted hair had started to come loose and was trailing a strand on her forehead. 'It hasn't been easy for me either. I'll be alone now. No support—'

He said, 'If you want me to, Mrs. Gowen, I can take some of this material. Some of his work. I have a son in graduate school—' He stopped. No use misleading vulnerable people more than—well, than the job required. 'I can read some of it. Perhaps mention it to someone I know at the morning paper. If you want me to.'

'I think so. That would be very nice.' She still held his fingers, but the grip had gone flabby. Spidery, he thought. 'And come to see me again. Will you?'

'If you want me to.'

'Let me know what the man at the newspaper says. What he thinks.'

'Yes.' She held his hand so lightly now he could barely feel it, and he moved his away.

'He had so much talent. So much. Please let me know what that editor says about his work.'

'Yes.'

CHAPTER SEVEN

Birge frequently accompanied his wife Edna to church—not regularly, since he often had to work or said he did—but often enough so that it satisfied her, so that the minister and her friends could see him and know who he was, so that she could not be classed with the widows, weekend or otherwise, whose husbands were dead or home watching football. The arrangement was unspoken; in return she did not drag him into discussions with the minister or others, or to Bible study or cake bakes, and she was grateful the rest of the week. She had her devotion, closely intertwined with a social life that gave many of the long hours she was without him meaning and direction. It was what she wanted. And when she had also wanted Roy to go to Sunday school and then to the clubs, and Roy hadn't seriously objected, Birge had thought, why not? He hadn't seen many delinquents brought in straight from a Methodist church.

Then why had he been so angry when the natural, if not inevitable, had occurred and Roy had quietly, but very definitely, told them that he and a girl he had met in church had decided that they wanted to get married and devote their lives to foreign missions? No, Roy said, they had made up their minds. They had had a call. They wanted to dedicate themselves to serve a higher purpose. Life was not just stuffing and breeding. They were firm and would not change.

'He's not even out of high school yet,' Birge shouted. 'He's not even eighteen!'

Looking back later it seemed probable that Edna was even more disturbed, under her apparent calm, than he was. She had certainly not wanted this, but how could she argue against it? If ever there was poetic justice . . . 'Have patience, Sam, and don't shout so loud. He *is* only a boy. Give him time.'

'Time!'

He did not have her conflicts, and there were balancing advantages to the situation he might also have considered. Under the circumstances it didn't seem likely that Roy was tupping that girl—who seemed quite a nice girl—or doing as much drinking and hell raising as his classmates. But none of this mollified him. 'Is this the way we want him to spend his life? Is this what we've worked for?'

Perhaps, as Edna urged, he should have let time take care of it. Perhaps, to some extent, time did. The enthusiasms and mistakes of youth are seldom binding unless you let yourself get locked into them. Every boy wants to be a ball player or a pilot or something like that; later he may want to try art, or mountain climbing, or some idealistic cause he may have picked up in church or from a frustrated school or gym teacher. But Birge had put on pressure, and years later still regretted it. Even if in the end it had probably not mattered.

The girl had gone to another school and then married someone else. Roy was now in graduate school in Colorado, and usually stayed West in the summers to work in a national park. He seemed happy enough, the infrequent times they saw him. Birge knew he was living with some woman—it wasn't hard for a detective to find out—whom he occasionally referred to vaguely in letters as 'a girlfriend.' They had never met her. Birge didn't think Edna knew, but she certainly suspected.

In his most recent letter Roy had said that, listening to the sober advice of practical people around him who had been out job hunting, he was seriously considering transferring over to the MBA program because there seemed to be more future 'moneywise' than in his present scientific field. Knowledgeable people earnestly warned him against continuing.

On the last visit home Birge had finally

brought himself to ask Roy what he thought now about that 'dedication to higher service.' Roy had laughed. Then they had been interrupted, and he had never really answered.

So it was all turning out 'all right.' And Birge's reaction had been way out of proportion. Why had he become so worked up because a teenage son had had a half-baked idea? Every teenager had, or had had, something like it—as a man who had been forced to drop out of college after his second year and then 'go on the cops' to earn a living well knew.

*　　*　　*

The nude pictures had been cut from photography magazines and were garnished underneath and along the margins with technical data about time of exposure, lens focal length, and size of aperture, as though those were the only, or major, reasons for reproduction. There was also some general artistic jargon about angle and direction of lighting, softness of focus, 'reflective surfaces,' shading, composition, posing for best effect. Wesley Gowen—Birge presumed it was he—had underlined some of the latter—items, Birge noted, that could most easily be translated into prose descriptions.

In most photos the ladies (if the purpose was only art, how come none were of men?) had their legs coyly raised or crossed, but the breasts were bare and prominent. Under one head-on, waist-up photo, Wesley (and this would certainly be he) had typed unevenly: 'Do the nipples really expand and change color during passion? I'll have to find out.' He hadn't known and so would have to find out. (Did Birge himself remember? He glared at Hagen—at his desk across the room, innocently whistling through his teeth as he finished some paperwork—as though Charley had asked the question.)

Hagen, feeling the eyes on him, looked up and saw what was on Birge's desk. 'Dirty pictures?'

'Art.'

'Yeah.'

The police attitude towards vice was, in its own way, remarkable. It assumed that the worst motivations were, in most cases, the ones to be expected, yet it was prepared to punish them as abnormal and shocking.

'They're from photography magazines. Art and technical stuff. Gowen had them in his files... You can buy them anywhere.'

'Yeah. I used to be very interested in that kind of photography.'

110

'Maybe we should take *you* in.' Birge spread them out before him. Not all the photographs were nudes. One was a colored page from some gardening magazine of spring flowers, with names underlined. 'He wanted to be a writer. And he didn't know everything.'

'Neither do we.' Hagen's eyes stayed on his superior for a while, then went back to his own work.

There was one major difficulty with that conventional, pessimistic police attitude: It was usually right. Statistics backed up that conclusion. He put the pictures back in the folder and began to read some of the typewritten notes and script—to supplement those he had spent over an hour reading the night before.

CHAPTER EIGHT

'The Journal of Wesley W. A. GOWEN.'

The 'Wesley' had been carefully slashed out, but apparently he had not thought that such an error or change of mind was reason enough to start a new page. Maybe journals were supposed to be spontaneous and heartfelt, including doubts as well as inspirations. Anyway, Gowen seemed to have decided what his professional name was to be, and that might be enough justification to preserve the page. Birge glanced down. Two other words were crossed out, both toward the bottom. Three-quarters was type-written; the bottom few lines were in script—blue ballpoint. Birge began to skim. The journal was kept in a three-hole high school notebook, and after that first page Gowen wrote on both sides of each, making some attempt to stay on the blue lines. After a few pages the text seemed to move more rapidly, the spacing and spelling to be less precise... It might, Birge thought, be a real find—but not, he had to add silently, for literary reasons...

DESCRIPTIONS

The street. It is a long and dark street. Or it seems long, because it just grows dark, it does not seem to have an end. Just a dark blank. This is partly because it is narrow, and the houses have no lawns and are close to the sidewalks. They are old houses—red brick with some kind of red stone arches and decorations above the doors and windows and on the corners—although the houses are so close that many don't have corners. Some have iron balconies, usually rusted, on the second floors, and some have fire escapes, angling down [a

112

space, indicating a pause, probably for thought] *like stitches on a wound . . .*

I usually park there when I drive, because there usually are not enough parking spaces on the lot that would not interfere with the trucks, and walk. Some of the windows are lit, and I sometimes glance in as I pass. I do not know them and they do not know me, so I think it is all right. I am not offending them. They are poor people, many of them are black, and I want to know how they live. What do they think and feel? Really feel? I have asked questions—trying to be careful—of the laborers on the platform, and they usually laugh or joke. They tell me that if I keep walking through that neighborhood I will get mugged or ripped off, but I have never been afraid. I will never be afraid, and I think they know it, because they have always been friendly when I met any and said hello, as though they were actually grateful, or rather happy, to speak. (There was just one exception: a fancily dressed man that Jerry calls 'Superfly,' but he's the only one.) I will never be afraid of the plain ordinary people of the American lower depths—'For oh the poor people, that are flesh of my flesh . . . when I see the iron hooked into their faces' (D. H. Lawrence, 'City Life').

The most interesting building—the one second from the corner, just a block south of work. I had seen long curtains on the first-floor windows—the old-fashioned lace kind, and the windows too are very high and old-fashioned, like the old mansions used to be—which moved sometimes as I walked by, and there were dim lights, and I heard something like whispers— whispers on the evening. But then twice, I saw men park and go inside—white men—and yesterday I stopped . . .

Birge glanced at the top of the page, and then flipped back a page, but there was no date on that entry, or the one that seemed to precede it.

. . . I stopped, and looked, and waited. The curtains spread a little, and there was a black girl's face. A little light right behind her. Her lips very red, and she looked as much oriental as black. I just stood and I caught her eyes. She smiled. She looked back, in my eyes. She tapped on the glass with her fingernail, or maybe a dime held in her fingers: not loud. She kept smiling—bright teeth, very bright—and she kept moving her finger toward the door, telling me to come in, I guess. But we looked in each other's eyes for over a minute. She quit smiling. Then she dropped the curtains. Maybe somebody called her, I don't know. I heard voices. Maybe she came to the door too, maybe

to entice me. Maybe what happened was that she saw that police car turning the corner, and the policeman looking at me . . .

Birge pulled his memo pad to him, started to write, then paused to shove a wrinkled carbon between the two top sheets, and started to write again.

RE: FYI
TO: Vice Squad, Attn: Cantrell, Lt.
FROM: Birge, Capt.
Information received routine homicide investigation indicates that whorehouse near corner Eighth and Mayberry may be operating again. Information reliable but may be dated.
COPY(IES) TO: Harrison, Maj., CD.
PERSONAL ATTN!

He tore the two sheets off and put them in his OUT tray. Cantrell knew damn well that place was operating, and those cops weren't even pretending not to know, but instead kept an eye on it for somebody's payoff. Now let's see what the chief of detectives' office does about it. He went back to his reading.

I want to go inside. I have only been in a place like that once, and then I only sat and talked to the older woman in the first room—the

115

madam—while the others went toward the back with the girls. I want to go in, to find that girl, to talk to her. I'll pay for her time, just to talk to her... Where was she from? What was her life like? What does she feel? Think? Who is she?

I don't think I will ever go into that house. But I think it will always be part of me, part of my mind, whenever I pass, almost every work night...

Birge frowned. Where did that kid get that kind of stuff, from his background? Had Roy been like that? No, certainly not, everyone was different. What about Birge, Sam, Capt.? Oh, that was ridiculous; those were different times. Besides—analyze the words—the kid hadn't really done anything, he hadn't even been with any whores—so what was so far out about him? But, of course, it wasn't really the whores, or what he actually did...

Birge began to turn the pages, reading a few words in each, looking for the first mention of the restaurant, or the people in it, or the apartments. He had over years and millions of pages of reports acquired the almost mystic belief that no matter how fast he went, his eye and mind would catch anything important. If he was wrong, nobody had yet found him out.

. . . I told her I would give her some money if she would use it for something good—not good for me, I meant, but good for her—and not if she was going to give it to him. She kept saying she wanted to go back to school, to make something of herself. I said . . .

Who? The whore? Birge had just found himself out. He went back a page, read a paragraph, then began to go farther back, reading more carefully. It was not the whore—or not that one anyway. He took down a name, and a street. He checked to see if there were any more. There was an approximate age. He dialed the records office and gave them what he had, instructing them to call as soon as they found anything. There had to be some kind of record, probably in the juvenile files. Yes, he *knew* about the confidentiality rule—'I told you this was Captain Birge!—who are you again?'—but this was a murder investigation. All right, he'd wait to be called back.

He went back to the journal, turning the pages more slowly. Other characters appeared. Wesley Gowen was starting to develop the episodes, describing faces and places, writing the conversations as dialogue, in separate paragraphs, as in vignettes or short stories. When the answer from records came, he carefully listed the information on his pad in his own semi-shorthand, thanked the clerk with more civility than he had shown before, put the slip in his pocket, and left. As he passed through the outer office, he felt only a trifle uneasy because he knew the department head shouldn't spend his time like this, shouldn't be going off on a tangent, on a minor lead. That's what Rodigault, sitting in the outer office and pretending to be typing reports, was there for. But he didn't think that anyone else in the office would know exactly what to ask—or even why he was interviewing this girl.

CHAPTER NINE

'Your name is Rosajoy Wilkerson,' Birge said.
    'Yessir.'
    'Rosajoy—is that one name or two?'
    'I usually spell it like one. But sometimes some spell it like two. Social workers—people like that.'
    Her hair had been frizzed, or overdyed, or something, and mostly floated like a blonde cloud around her head; one pink curler held down a little on the left side, but she either hadn't had time to put in more or hadn't

bothered. Her face was young, round, and her features were soft—except that her nose had apparently once been damaged, and was bent to the left. Her eyes were large and cautious—but she was more quietly apprehensive than frightened. He guessed that she was accustomed to sitting calmly, no matter how she felt, when any official addressed her. And probably blanking out everything he said.

'I want to talk to you about personal things. Maybe we ought to be alone.'

The boyfriend was in the room. He had apparently awakened when he heard Birge's voice, because he had been scratching himself and his hair was tousled when he had come in—it was, after all, only noon. Because of the precipitate way he had entered, and then as precipitately stopped and sat down, Birge suspected that he knew a cop when he saw one. He wore tight and torn blue jeans and little else—one brown sock dangled from a foot. Birge stared at him, assuming that he would get the message, but he stared back blankly.

She said, 'I guess, sir, you wanted to ask about Wes Gowen?'

Birge's eyebrows raised. 'Yes. How did you know?'

The man was scratching the sparse hairs on his thin and partially sunken chest. He had

119

slid down until he was almost off the chair. He said, 'What's all that about, hon?' His eyes stayed on Birge.

'It's about a boy I used to know.' She could hardly have been older than Gowen; was probably a year or more younger. Her voice assumed a whining note. 'You remember about it, sugar.'

'No, I don't.'

'Why, yes you do. It was that young boy I met at the Red Cat about a year ago. That funny one. You know. You were working ... well, up north then, but I told you about him when you came back.'

She had been up and in the kitchen when Birge had pressed the bell, but it could not have been long; she still wore pajama tops above her pedal pushers, and the coffee was only just starting to simmer. The grease-stained box from last night's pizza—he hoped it was last night's—was on the floor, and the remnants of the pizza along with the dishes were in the sink.

'Oh yeah,' the boyfriend said. 'Him.' He grinned briefly, showing stained teeth.

'How did you know?' Birge repeated.

'Well, I read something in the paper last night ... Well, I *did*, sugar. That's what I was reading last night while you were talking to those fellas in the bowling alley. That's

120

what I was doin'. I didn't go out anywhere.'

The young man's eyes now moved to her, and held hers for a moment. He didn't answer. He kept scratching, and his chest developed a red streak. She licked her lips, and her eyes lowered.

'Well, he's dead. As you know.'

'That's why you came. Wasn't nothing else?'

'Nothing else.'

'Well, I didn't have nothin' to do with it.'

'I got your name from . . . a kind of journal he kept.'

'Well, he didn't have no right to do anything like that.'

Birge started to say, as though it explained anything, that Wesley had wanted to be a writer, but he stopped, because he thought that such information would convey nothing to her. She had raised her eyes and was looking at him blankly. He noticed, as the hazy sun through the one window hit it, that not only was the curler pink but the fuzz of hair around it.

'I'm just trying to get background information now. You're not being accused of anything.'

'Yuh had to go out and start something, didn't you . . . Rosie?' the boyfriend said. He had obviously intended to use a stronger term than her name.

The boyfriend would have to be neutralized quickly. 'I'm Detective Captain Sam Birge, from headquarters. We haven't been introduced yet. What's your name?'

The other quit scratching his chest and straightened up slowly. Birge sat impassively, his eyes lying steadily, like mild weights, on the youth. After a moment of pretend defiance and a stutter, Birge got a name. He pretended to write it carefully on his pad. He didn't have to, nor would he have to check the record—probably first came to the attention of authorities as a runaway, or branded 'incorrigible' by mother; a series of detention centers for juveniles or maybe foster homes; arrests and pickups starting around thirteen, probably originally for shoplifting or stealing from newsstands or slot machines; graduated to liquor store break-ins and other petty thefts, running with a gang, and 'hustling the queers'—male prostitution in legal jargon; and so on, to his present exalted state of living on this girl's earnings and unemployment checks while he looked around for greater opportunities. Most young men with such backgrounds outgrew the overt crime, if not the scars, by his age—but he hadn't. They understood one another. He would not interrupt Birge, or openly try to terrorize the girl again—while the detective was there, at least.

He turned back to the girl. 'Please understand me, Miss Wilkerson. I have nothing against you now. I just want to find out more about Wesley Gowen. What kind of person he was, and so on. You knew him. I expect cooperation.'

She had heard that tone of voice before. It was probably a regular part of her life. 'Yes sir.'

'Then tell me how you met him and what happened.'

'Well, I was working in this nightclub. It's called the Red Cat Club.'

'I know the place. What did you do there?'

'I was a waitress.'

If she had been a waitress at all, it was part-time. Most of the time she would be hustling the male customers—they were almost all male; salesmen passing through for some reason seemed to like to go there, in bunches—and, since her figure, from what he could see of it, was not yet entirely gone, she would every couple of hours or less take her turn for a few minutes in a small roped-off section of the floor that served as a stage, stripping slowly with her back to an extremely bored black combo, and intoning in a flat nasal drawl the words to some dirty tune that they were presumably playing. If she still worked there she would age quickly.

'You still work there?'

'No. Lonnie made me quit. I'm workin' some at the Taco Hut.'

Probably didn't want you putting it out for nothing, Birge thought. He sighed silently. He was getting as bad as Hagen. Even if it was true.

'Well, tell me about Wesley Gowen.'

She glanced quickly at Lonnie, and then, as quickly, lowered her glance to her lap, on which her hands were clenched tight. Lonnie was staring at her under lowered brows. Birge said, very quietly, 'Are you two married?'

The question surprised her so that she did not look first at the younger man for cues. 'Oh, no.'

'Yes we are,' Lonnie said. He was, or thought he was, a little sharper.

'You are?'

'Practically. We're going to have the ceremony right away. Soon's we get the blood test through and all that stuff... It's almost the same thing.'

'Legal rights and responsibilities don't come without the ceremony and certification. I'm not sure you're supposed to be here.' The poker player again, with no real legal cards in his hand. It would probably have been easier, and more honest, to simply order him out, as Hagen would have done—also without a legal pretense.

'Well, that . . . common law, they call it—well, that gives me rights.'

It was easy to win a bluff with an experienced player who immediately became rattled and made dumb moves. Still, for the kind of punk he was, he did show nerve to stand up to a police captain this way . . . Would he have done it to a tougher cop, like Hagen?

'Seven years together required in this state,' Birge said. 'She would have been a minor. And a very young one.' The words, and his eyes, gathered weight on the youth for a moment. 'I think you can find your shirt and shoes, and then something to do outside until we're finished here. Go ahead. I don't have much time.'

When Lonnie had gone out—quietly—Birge said to the girl, 'Go ahead. As I said, I don't have much time. When did you first meet him?'

'Well, it was that night—I don't know exactly when—'

'All right.'

'He came in late with two other fellas, I guess from where he works. We weren't doin' much, close to closing. It was after hours.' She stopped; her eyes grew round and frightened again; she had made a terrible mistake, in front of a policeman . . .

'Go on. You haven't commited any crimes yet.' Few people, and that unfortunately included the police, wanted to enforce the closing-time law. And it wasn't his province anyway. Or he would have enforced it.

'Well, they were sitting alone, and we weren't doing much, and the boss said what you sittin' around for, go keep them boys company.' Again she stopped, again the fear—and this time she had actually said something incriminating—and waited.

'Go ahead. I'm only interested in finding out about Gowen.'

'Well, you know . . . we ordered drinks. You know. And there was laughing.' She paused. 'One of the fellas put his hand under Gloria's dress. And she said stop it. We was about to leave anyway. He said the drinks was too expensive, and, you know, he wouldn't buy any more unless he got something for it. And the boss was watching anyway. That time of night, fellas like that, you got to expect some trouble.'

'What about Gowen? Was that all that happened?'

'No. He told the other fella to stop, he shouldn't treat us like that, it was our work. I

126

was surprised. The other fella called him names.'

'What names?' What did his fellow workers think of him?

'I don't remember everything. Jerk, and wet pants—that's a funny name, isn't it? And why were they so dumb to take a punk like him along? That's when the third fellow began to argue with the first, and he got real mad.

'I knew Gloria was having her period and was weak from . . . things . . . anyway. You know. So . . . I yelled at him that he was a big bully and to let her alone.' She explained: 'You got to do that sometimes to stop them. And to break it up too. I got a pretty big mouth, so I do it.'

Birge nodded. 'Go ahead. Maybe a little faster.'

'I was lookin' at the boss. I saw him wave at Mike—that's the bartender, he has some kind of bohunk name, but we call him Mike—and Mike reachin' down under the bar. And I shouldn've been lookin' that way because I didn't watch the guy makin' the trouble, and then my head kind of exploded and I couldn't see anything and my nose was hurtin' awful.' She answered his unspoken question by holding out her arm like a stiff-arming fullback, palm straight up and the heel thrust forward hard. 'He did that.'

127

'Is that what happened to your nose?'

'Well, I had most of that before. A ... accident I had. But I guess he helped.'

'Go on.'

'I couldn't see anything. I was bleedin' all over the table, and Gloria was screamin'. I thought I sort of saw, on the edge, that third fella and Wes grabbin' that bastard under the arms and hustlin' him away, an' I think I heard the boss hollerin'. But that can't be really right—unless a lot of time passed— because I was still cryin' an' I felt cold and wet against my face and that nose hurtin'. What happened was that Wes had a handkerchief full of ice from the glasses, and was holdin' it against my nose and tellin' me to hol' my head back. An' the boss was hollerin' loud as he could, "Git outta here you sunvabitch or I'll freeze your ass in jail for the rest of your life!" I don't remember everything, but I remember that pretty clear.' She had been absorbed by her recital: her fingers had quit fidgeting on the table, and her eyes had been staring, as though watching the events, over his shoulder. Now suddenly the frightened look came back to them, and she glanced at Birge quickly and then looked down. 'The boss knows a couple of police lieutenants good. Takes them back in his office when they come in.'

Birge sighed. 'Go ahead. Just stick to Wesley.'

'He took me home.'

'Wesley did?'

'The girls helped. I couldn't see nothin', I was still hurtin'. It was time almost to quit, and Gloria went too. The boss let her. Wes took a cab an' paid for it. You see, those fellas took the car he came in.' She paused. 'I don't know much what happened the rest of that night, once I got home. Gloria gave me some Darvon pills—well, she keeps them for female cramps and things, you know . . .'

He had a pretty good idea that she did not get those pills on a legal prescription—and they might not all have been Darvon—but he just said, 'Go on.'

'I was bombed out of my skull, I guess. I took them for the pain, you know, but I was bombed out. I woke up, it must have been noon, and I was pretty groggy. Wes was still there.'

'Where?'

'There. In a chair. Waiting for me to wake up, he said. I don't know if he ever got in the bed at all. I was still wearing my dress, and I examined myself, and I don't think anything happened at all, that time. Bombed out, you can't always tell.'

'How long did you go with him? Or

129

know him?'

'I don't know. Some time, though not always steady. I used to still see him sometimes even after Lonnie came back. He's a very funny fella.'

'How do you mean? Did he do anything strange?'

'I guess. He used to ask me things like did it feel good that time, and what could he do to make it better for me. Could he get me things. Things like that. Used to make me feel weird. I don't know why he was hangin' around me. He could have had lots of girls . . . from his own neighborhood.'

'Did he try to introduce you to any more of his friends?'

'I guess not. He did come to some of our parties, but he didn't drink much. He would hang around the Red Cat Club sometimes, after work, and buy drinks there, though they cost much more.'

'Did he ever take you to a place called Petit Montmartre?'

'Once.' Her eyes shifted.

'What happened?'

'Nothing.'

'Nothing at all?'

'No . . . it was just kind of weird.'

'Didn't he introduce you to anybody?'

'No. Or I don't remember. I don't . . .

know places like that.' She sighed. 'I ast him a couple of times—why do you hang around? You come from a nice family an' all. I was goin' with Lonnie, an' I was afraid there was goin' to be a fight. And he'd've been hurt. You know, this kid . . . Lonnie's a different kind of fella.' Then again, as suddenly, the eyes were frightened. 'But Lonnie didn't have anything to do with it! He never even really met him!'

'All right . . . About Wesley—do you think he wanted anything unusual? Do you think he might have been homosexual or something like that?'

'I don't know. Maybe not. Not usual queer.' Her gaze, again over his shoulder, was rapt. She smiled—a somewhat crooked grimace, her left upper lip lifting over a canine turning gray. 'I finally told him not to come around anymore. And then a few days later I come home with Lonnie an' I see him standin' just in the doorway an' the rain is really comin' down. Pourin'! I thought I'd die. Lucky Lonnie didn't know him for sure, must've thought he was some other apartment. So I went inside—he didn't say nothin'—told Lonnie to wait, I forgot somethin', be right back, an' came out, thinkin' maybe he got the message. But he was still there, soaked. So I said, "What you think you're doin'? I *told* you to stay away! I'm no *good* for you! Or anybody!" He just says, "I don't care. You can't be happy with a man like that. If I give you some money, will you go back to school, study for a better job?" Now can you beat that?'

Birge did not answer. He heard footsteps—trying to be as noiseless as possible. Then the door quivered a little—as, probably, Lonnie pressed his ear against it.

Birge asked, 'Do you think there was something wrong with him psychologically?'

She looked at him blankly. He said, 'Never mind. Why do you suppose he acted like that?'

'I don't know. Well, you ast about queer. You meet all kinds. One time—we didn't go to bed together much, just a few times—he ast me could we leave the light on for just a couple minutes. I thought, well, here comes the weird part. I ast why. He said he just wanted to watch my nipples for a minute or two. If I didn't mind. Not the usual queer, but a very funny fella.'

*   *   *

Back at the office, after listening with some impatience, Hagen said, 'What about that drug bit?'

132

'What drug bit?'

'Right there.' Hagen flipped a few pages and jabbed a forefinger at a pencil-marked paragraph ... So Hagen had been going through the journal too. Well, routine police work—wouldn't have been doing his job if he hadn't. No way to keep him—a good cop—from it.

... he was very angry. He said, 'Who told you that lie? Where you comin' from, man?' I told him that I would pay him the price of what they call a nickel bag—that is, $5—every day, at least for a while, if he would just not sell to her ...

Birge thought: So that was, probably, where he got that scar ... To Hagen he said, 'Forget it.'

CHAPTER TEN

PROGRESS REPORT
RE: GOWEN, W. Hom. file # G4584
TO: Birge, S., Capt., Hom. Div.
FROM: Hutkin, R., Pr. Ptlman (Spec. Assgnmt.)
Arrived as directed restaurant-bar Petit

Montmartre, 3412 Evergreen St.,
11:58 P.M., 4/24. . . .

It hadn't been all that precise, of course, but it
had been close to midnight, and Hutkin knew
that the PD, like all the organizations with
which he had been associated since boyhood—
the schools, the county courthouse where Pa
worked, the Marines—all liked 'exact' data in
their reports, even if not entirely 'correct.'
Gave them—and him—a handle on reality, a
feeling of at least partial control. Even Captain
Birge in his lectures at the police academy had
emphasized accuracy—which wasn't exactly
the same as precision, but close enough. He
had never yet read a report that was really
complete or really 'accurate.' But some were
close enough to pass.

On entering, observed subjects Brodovic
and De Plaissy sitting together alone at
table in SE corner of floor. They
immediately motioned to me to join
them. . . .

He hadn't been accurate, of course, when
he said that he had only come to the restaurant
two or three times before the night of the
murder, but it seemed obvious that Captain
Birge understood that—and had done nothing

134

about it though he was tough enough on other things—so that was all right. No harm done. When he had said that he knew Jeanne De Plaissy well enough so that 'sometimes' she sat and visited with him—that certainly put the lie to his 'two, three times'—the captain must have caught that too.

Well, he had also said that the proprietor had hardly ever spoken to him except as a businessman to a customer... Yet there the man was, smoking his pipe, grandly waving Hutkin in toward him and indicating an empty chair to his right with a hospitable—if abrupt and commanding—gesture.

Jeanne was also smiling—wanly, but with welcome—and that, apart from his orders, was enough to bring him over. That skinny girl with the stringy hair—the one they called Millie—was standing by Jeanne's chair trying vehemently to get some point across—she was always vehement—but Jeanne, with a whisper, got her to leave (she glared at Hutkin before she did) as he approached.

Brodovic shoved out the chair next to him and pointed to it; so that was where he had to sit—across from Jeanne rather than next to her.

She said, 'Thought you might be here last night. Then I was afraid you might never come again. Or that they held you.'

'No. I just had to make up some work.' He had actually had to go to his precinct to report and tell them of his new assignment, and that jerk behind the desk, Sgt. Chrisman, though he must have had the orders in the unread pile before him, said he didn't believe a word of it and they'd had to call headquarters. Then he still had to go ahead and work part of his shift, until the lieutenant who was in charge gave him special permission to go home.

She didn't look as though she had slept much: cheeks drawn, underside of the eyes dark and puffy.

'Where you work?' Brodovic asked.

'City job.' He didn't want to lie any more than he had to. 'Civil service.' But Brodovic did not question him further; the answer had provided a convenient square classification, and he nodded.

'What the police ask you?'

'The same thing they asked everybody, I guess. Did I know the fellow that was killed—what was his name—Wesley Gowen?'

'Yes,' Jeanne said, 'that was it. What did you say?'

'I couldn't remember ever having seen him before. I don't, though they say he was around here a lot.'

'A few times,' Brodovic said. 'Not many.'

Jeanne gave Brodovic a long, slow look,

136

then turned back toward Hutkin. 'He was around quite a bit. More than you. I'm surprised you didn't see him.'

'Well, I don't remember him.' He waited to see if they would say any more. Perhaps he hadn't been too bright in his answers. Jeanne was regarding him levelly, perhaps waiting for something more. 'Could I have seen him walking through? Maybe going upstairs?'

Brodovic raised his eyebrows and turned toward her. 'He came up,' she said, 'sometimes with the group.'

'A terrible thing,' Brodovic said. 'Police in the hall all morning, taking pictures, talking loud. And people coming around.' He shrugged. 'I thought they would be coming here, asking, "Is this the place that young man was killed?" You know—what kind of place is this? Terrible!'

Hutkin had a feeling that he would have preferred that to the way the place was now: Millie arguing intensely with a young couple dressed and speaking something like her; two young men in sport coats working over a chessboard surrounded by beer bottles; a young man sitting close beside and whispering to an overdressed woman older than he was; and all the other tables empty.

'Is that all you can think of?' De Plaissy asked.

Brodovic kept looking at her, then shrugged. 'He was a very unlucky boy. It is a very sad thing. But he is not one of ours.' His pipe was clogged; he took it out of his mouth and tapped it.

She was crying. Hutkin saw no change in her expression or demeanor, and he might have gone on, sitting and chatting as they had before, except that she turned her head suddenly—probably to keep Brodovic from noticing—and the candlelight flickered and turned in the tears of her lids and her eyes. None were yet on her face. She probably thought that in a moment or two she could turn back, her face under control, and no one would know.

'Did the police ask you anything about me? Or Jeanne?' Brodovic asked.

'Just how many times I came here, and did I meet you or know you.' That was safe enough. 'I said I didn't come much and it was all casual.' Now to shift the focus to a less dangerous and more relevant—to the police—subject: 'It *is* a terrible thing about that fellow Gowen. Who was he? Does anybody know what happened?'

Brodovic's pipe was working again. He nodded toward Jeanne. 'Ask her.'

She turned toward Hutkin—slowly, shielding her face partly from the candle on

138

the table—and from Brodovic. But she had control of that face and he could no longer see tears. 'He was just a very nice young boy that came around to talk. And I guess to enjoy himself. Like you.' Now she did look directly at Brodovic. 'And I *don't* know what happened. Any more than Mirko.' She raised those eyes to the ceiling and said quietly, 'Oh, my God!'

'Well—' Hutkin started to speak, then stopped. He did not want to pursue the matter and was afraid he might antagonize them into silence and perhaps even into having nothing else to do with him (that might be a good reason to give the captain for not charging ahead). Still, he had to get the information some way... 'Well, it's ... I guess a pretty bad situation. The police coming around; nobody knows what's going to happen next; people asking me questions down at work... I guess the people upstairs are pretty worried too, aren't they?' His throat was dry. I'm a pretty lousy actor, he thought... He made a sympathetic gesture toward Brodovic and started again: 'Customers too, I guess?'

Brodovic drummed his blunt fingertips on the table; they sounded like small fists. 'We didn't do anything! Why should *we* suffer?'

'You don't quite understand Mirko,' Jeanne De Plaissy said. Her voice was soft and

139

absolutely flat. 'Mirko's not really interested in money for itself. Just in what serves his "art". Or gets in its way.'

Perhaps because he was sensitive to it, whether the situations were exact or not, Hutkin got the cold feeling that used to come to his stomach when his parents had fought. Except that there were no tears or shouting or whinning, just the cold.

In a moment Brodovic sighed and tapped his pipe on the large, black ashtray that he kept only on this table, leaving ash and some sparks in the bowl. The bell to the front door had rung. He said, 'I have to see to the customers,' pushed himself up, and moved off. His voice came back to them from the door, hearty and strong, no tremor: 'Hello! Please come in!'

A middle-aged couple—the man with suit and tie, the woman wearing a cocktail dress and imitation pearl earrings—looking around a little uncertainly. Some friends of theirs had recommended the place, the man said, but they weren't sure . . .

'Not at all, not at all! Glad you could come. This table here would be fine, I think!' He sat them against the wall, a substantial distance from Millie, and motioned toward the waitress, who had been leaning against the back wall, to take their order. Then he turned again to the door, to greet an entering group from the university. Business was better, might actually be good in time, despite everything.

She said, 'I have to finish up some work now. Why don't you come up, say, in half or three-quarters of an hour? We can talk. Some other friends will be there.'

From the argument at the near table he was afraid he knew what friends those would be. But he nodded, smiled, and said, 'Sure.'

'It won't be a lesson,' she said. 'There won't be any charge.'

CHAPTER ELEVEN

Coming up the last few steps, Hutkin could see the spot where the body had lain, gradually revealed and then almost vivid before him, because its worn linoleum tiles had been scrubbed while the rest of the hall had not. His path went around it, to Jeanne's door.

He was about to knock, and a voice to his right said, 'Hey!' He turned. The man he had seen standing close to the body—dirty T-shirt, torn jeans, two girlfriends—was advancing toward him, grinning, holding a bottle of wine—a cheap brand. The T-shirt had been replaced by a blue-checked flannel shirt with its tails hanging out and the socks by torn moccasins—and only one girlfriend was with him. He held up the bottle. 'You're supposed to bring your own,' he said. 'Otherwise you have to go downstairs and pay Mirko's prices. Free is bad for business.'

'You going in here?'

'Sure. Your first time?'

'No.' It was, but that was none of his business.

'I only been a few times myself. I ain't part of that kind of scene. But this time I thought it might be interesting.' He waved the bottle to emphasize his previous point. 'You got something better?'

'I just drink tea,' Hutkin said, and knocked. While he waited for the answer the thought struck him that, since he obviously was not carrying any sizeable bottle, the man might have been referring to drugs, and he should have followed that lead . . . But maybe he shouldn't; he was here for something else, and it was a little too early to drop his cover. He had noticed the smell of pot on the clothes of some of the people he had seen in the restaurant and upstairs, but he hadn't seen anyone actually light up . . . Peace, Hutkin . . .

142

A bolt was shot, the door was yanked open, and Millie was staring out at him—that harsh stare with enlarged irises. She was probably wearing contacts, he thought, a little uneasily. Before either could speak, a voice behind her said, 'Come on in,' and the flannel shirt again said, 'Hey!' and pushed past both of them.

The room, though not great, was larger than he had expected, running from the hall to the outside wall in the back, and including all of the apartment space except the bedroom and a small bath to the left, and an alcove kitchen behind a curtain, also to the left. Jeanne De Plaissy was at a drawing table close to the two windows—the only windows—in the back wall, on her high stool, smiling at him—or at them, since her eyes flickered over the flannel shirt and his companion before coming to rest on Hutkin. The smile, like the one she had given him downstairs, was brief and tired, 'Glad you could make it'—as though he had come a long distance at great trouble.

'Harold shoved in,' Millie said, aggrieved, motioning toward the flannel shirt. 'You might expect it.'

'Well, he's welcome. Hello, Harold.' And, to his female companion, 'And Sadie.'

'Beautiful like always,' Harold said to Millie, and tried to pinch her, but she stepped

143

back quickly. He said, 'Haw!' twice, and pulled Sadie behind him towards some sofa cushions on the floor close to Jeanne.

Hutkin never did quite know who was there, since not all identified themselves. Millie's two friends had come with her; despite their Millie-like appearance they turned out to be an innocuous married couple named Hurwitz, from the university, whose major contributions to the conversation were to occasionally murmur polite modifications to Millie's more emphatic statements. A very thin young black man—who turned out to be one of De Plaissy's students—stood directly behind her, never taking his eyes off her work, and never uttering a single word all the time Hutkin was there. A rather elegant young man whose glasses' rims, soft mustache, and shirt all seemed to be the same blond-to-gold color, sat upright in a chair toward the center of the room and did most of the talking. 'Well it's not anything *we* could have prevented,' he said. 'I don't see why we should let it spoil everything.'

Jeanne had a large colored photograph of a flowering bush (blue hydrangeas, he thought—his mother had had some—but he wasn't sure) thumbtacked to a display board above her table, and she was making a stylized quick sketch of some of the flowers in pencil, perhaps preparatory to coloring them, since she had an open watercolor box on the side. She nodded vaguely when the blond mustache stopped speaking, and kept on with her work. The black youth moved closer to her shoulder. Without looking up she said, 'Hello, Ralph. Just take a seat anywhere.'

He took his seat toward the rear of the room—also on a cushion against the wall—close to the door on the left that apparently led to the bedroom. Millie and her friends were just ahead of him.

'Well, what are we going to do?' Millie said. Her voice rose at the end of the question. 'Pretend he didn't exist? It didn't happen?'

'Oh, we're sailing off on the guilt trip,' Harold said. 'The grand tour. That's wonderful.' He seemed elated. Sadie, her legs crossed and leaning against the wall, smiled faintly.

'Your usual nasty self,' Millie said. 'Enjoying nastiness. Even murder?'

'Millie,' Jeanne said. She erased part of a curve with a gum eraser and then filled it in again more carefully.

'*We* didn't do it, Millie,' the blond mustache said. 'It was a very bad thing. But unfortunate things happen every day. If we read in the paper that he had been killed in an accident—or somebody we didn't know,

145

somebody who was just as worthwhile a person, but somebody we never met—'

'Oh, rich,' Harold said, 'rich, rich!'

'But we did know him!' Millie cried. 'He was with us! A terrible thing—'

'*I* didn't know him,' Harold said. 'I saw him once or twice. He was one of these mice. He never said a word.' The blond mustache nodded slowly, apparently reluctant to be on the same side as Harold but anxious to make the same point, to keep the same distance.

'We always think we're so safe. But this happened to one of us! Right here, in this hall! What kind of world is it?' Millie shouted. Mrs. Hurwitz sighed sympathetically and her husband murmured a placating agreement.

'You mean that because we live in a poor neighborhood there are evil, mean people out there? That some big black druggie—' Harold's eyes fixed on the youth behind Jeanne's chair, and for the first time his voice acquired an uncertain note and trailed off. The young black man showed no sign of having noticed. Jeanne had taken a brush and was quickly stroking in gray shading behind the sketched flowers, and the young man was watching. Hutkin thought the corner of his mouth might have twitched a little.

But Millie's distress had changed to fury. 'Now don't you dare lay racism on me,

146

Harold! Everybody here knows me and don't you dare do that! You can *really* be nasty! You know. I mean it's the kind of world where, even here, nobody can ever really feel safe or sure anymore—' She waved her hands.

'Harold,' Jeanne said mildly. She wiped her brush after dipping it into some water. 'We're all friends here.'

The black youth still seemed unperturbed. He pointed at a spot on the sketch as though asking a silent question, and Jeanne nodded. Harold relaxed and smiled. 'Right.'

'I think the trick—the thing—in a situation like this is not to take everything too personal,' the blond mustache said. 'Everybody dies. And it's not as though he was a member of the family or anything like that. He was a nice fellow, and I think those of us who knew him best will miss him. But— you know—my own father died only about six months ago.' He paused. 'Well, I don't think you heard me say . . . much about it.'

'Was he murdered?' Millie shouted. 'Was he young?'

Mrs. Hurwitz muttered once more, and look distressed. Mr. Hurwitz said, 'But every parent's death is important to the children, Millie . . . I'm . . . really sorry, Spencer. You have our sympathy.'

'But I think that's just my point,' blond

147

mustache said. 'You see, when you think about it . . . see it in perspective—then you have to realize—'

'Oh crap!' Millie said. 'Crap, crap! And I could use a stronger word!'

'Well, go ahead, Millie,' Harold said. 'Don't hold back now. Gee whillickers!' This time Sadie smiled more broadly.

'It doesn't sound like . . .' Hutkin said, and paused because his words seemed to reverberate loud and strange in that room and to hang in the air. But he had to finish, '. . . sound like anybody knew him very well.' He waited for an answer almost anxiously, as though he had said something improper. And in a polite gathering.

He got his response. Millie stared at him. Blond mustache almost turned. Jeanne, for the first time since he had entered the room, looked up. Her eyes met his for a moment before they returned slowly to her work.

'Who?' Harold asked innocently.

Embarrassment quickly moved to anger. The bastard's trying to needle me, Hutkin thought. But by the time he had opened his mouth he had cooled down. He wasn't supposed to be a cop prepared to straighten a wiseassed witness out, but, probably, the kind of dumb, eager hanger-on Harold thought he was playing with. The fact that Harold kept

148

thinking that—and that Hutkin knew he wasn't and would have his own innings later— was warming. 'Wesley Gowen,' he said. He imagined that his eyes *were* unusually wide. 'Isn't that who we were talking about?' He turned toward Harold. The face above the stained blue flannel did look unusually pleased.

Before Harold could answer—if he intended to—Hutkin noticed that the door closest to him was opening silently. There was no light in the room beyond that he could see, just shadow. Or maybe a very dim amber, some kind of night light. Jeanne De Plaissy, who had been able to ignore most of the outcries, raised her head and turned. She said, 'Oh my goodness!'

Hutkin—and the others—all looked back toward the door. A boy stood in it, with rumpled dark hair and blue-striped pajamas. About ten, Hutkin thought. But the face looked older than that. Well, then a small twelve, maybe.

'Did we wake you up, darling?' Jeanne said. Her face looked genuinely distressed. 'Oh, isn't that too bad.'

The Hurwitzes murmured sorrows. 'Well,' the husband said, 'maybe we better go,' and the wife nodded.

'Oh no,' Jeanne said, 'he usually sleeps

right through everything. He's used to our sessions out here. I wonder if there's anything wrong. Come here, sweetheart.'

From the boy's eyes—Hutkin was the closest—it did not look to him as though the child had slept at all. Perhaps simply lain quietly, listening, as he stood quietly now. Then he walked toward his mother, not looking or speaking to the others—a strange small erect figure, with only the spiky hair stubbornly childlike.

He stopped before his mother. She took his arms and looked closely into his eyes, speaking softly but audibly, since the others were quiet. 'You feeling all right, sweetheart?'

He nodded. She put a palm to his forehead to check, and then used it to brush back his hair. She leaned forward to kiss him. 'You want to go to the bathroom?' He shook his head. At that age Hutkin had once thrown a tantrum when his mother had asked him a question something like that before others; but either the child didn't care or was oblivious, or very accustomed, to those in the room.

They whispered together a moment. Then Hutkin heard her say, 'But you'll have to get some sleep to go to school tomorrow.'

And for the first time Hutkin heard the

boy's voice: 'No school tomorrow. Remember?' It was a calm voice, rather flat, still a little high.

'Oh that's right! You told me, and I did forget. Well ... all right, honey, you want to sit out here for a while? But then you will have to go to bed.'

'I really think we ought to all go.' Mrs. Hurwitz said it this time.

'Not unless you want to. He's used to people. When he wants to go to sleep or to bed he'll simply go. Millie remembers. Right, honey?'

The boy had sat down at Jeanne's feet, half under the drawing table, as in a small cave. He looked out calmly and somberly at them, his arms around his shins.

'Hello, Gene,' Millie said, smiling for the first time.

For Hutkin's benefit, Jeanne said, 'His name is really Jean'—she gave it the French pronunciation—'not Eugene. But everybody at school pronounces it that way, and he doesn't say anything because he thinks it sounds more American.' She smiled. The boy moved his eyes from Millie to Hutkin, and made no comment. 'Jean and Jeanne, the comedy team,' his mother said. 'Yes, I know it's a lousy rhyme.' She went back to her work, but there was a small smile at the corner

151

of her mouth.

Millie tried to return to the main subject, but in a way that she apparently hoped would be over the boy's head. 'You never know what terrible thing is going to happen next. It's like living in a Dali painting. It makes no sense at all.'

'That's surrealism, not existentialism, Millie,' blond mustache explained.

'What?'

'I didn't mean to correct you, but you got the two mixed up, and they shouldn't be. Each has its own values.'

'Harold,' Jeanne said without taking her eyes from her work, 'you brought that bottle for something, didn't you?'

Harold raised the bottle aloft as though he had never seen it before. 'Oh yeah. Sure did. Brought it so's I wouldn't have to pay Brod's prices.'

'Don't worry about that.' She put down one brush, lifted another. 'Jean sweetheart, would you go get the glasses out, and pass one around to everyone? Would you?'

As silently as he had sat, the boy rose, passed through the curtains that cut off the kitchen alcove, and returned with a tray of glasses. He stopped before each guest and waited until a glass was taken, and then moved to the next. When they were gone he returned the tray to the kitchen and as silently went back to his place under the drawing table.

Harold, after pouring a good deal for himself and Sadie, started the bottle around. By the time it got to Hutkin, there were only a few drops in it. For a moment he thought of going downstairs to buy one—maybe two— more; he could charge it to expenses and be repaid, the first time he had ever had that privilege. But he would always wonder what he had missed while gone, and perhaps have to explain that to Birge, so he poured those drops into his glass and swished them around as though he had something. Lousy wine anyway, the kind winos drink.

Play Sherwood Forest, Hutkin said to himself, and smiled like an old-time cop. A department joke, based on the story— probably true—about the young church social worker who had told a beat cop ecstatically that some young delinquents she was working with were so reformed they had said they were going to the park to play Sherwood Forest— they really meant they had gotten hold of some bottles of Robin Hood brand wine and would get drunk and hang from trees and molest passersby . . .

The conversation went on, but at first the boy's presence, however silent, seemed to have provided a damper, because it was not as lively. It moved from the murder to art—could a desperate and horrible act (or life itself, as Millie insisted) really be portrayed in a painting so as to get its full message across? Spencer asked whether they could say that there was, properly speaking, such a thing as a truly existential painting. He wasn't trying to start an argument, he insisted, he had only asked for the sake of discussion. Let's consider Goya as a possibility . . .

In time, though, the boy seemed to be forgotten, because the arguments—they were hardly discussions—heated up, or at least they became more irritable as fatigue set in. Hutkin became bored and lost track for a while, but he sat up when he heard Millie shout that Harold couldn't really *know* what the killing had meant to anybody because he couldn't really *feel* anything—and Harold answered that feeling was cheap, but he *knew* because he had some facts!

'What?'

'That's for me to say.'

And for me, Hutkin thought with some satisfaction, and made a mental note to include it in his report. He looked around to see how the exchange had struck the others, but they did not seem to consider it essentially different from any of the other extreme statements. Jeanne's attention was somewhere else; her design was apparently finished, at least for the time being, and she was showing it to the black youth behind her who, his jacket already on, was making final notes or sketches. He finished and left; as he passed, Hutkin nodded to him and he nodded back, but without speech. Hutkin turned back to Jeanne and saw that the boy, under the table, was fast asleep, sitting up in those wrinkled pajamas, leaning against his mother's leg.

Time to break it up ... Hutkin moved forward and tapped Mrs. Hurwitz, as his most likely ally, and pointed to the child.

She said, 'Oh my,' whispered to her husband and pointed in her turn. He nudged Millie, stood up, tried to straighten his hopeless trousers, and told De Plaissy in a lowered voice, 'Thanks for everything, Jeanne, but we really do have to be going. Early classes.'

'Tender-hearted Millie,' Harold said for his parting shot, 'big help, wasn't it?' But he too made preparations to leave.

Hutkin came over to Jeanne to see if he could be of any help. She was making a final touch on the design, turning out a blue petal as though a breeze had just caught it. It was beautiful; he stopped in admiration before speaking. Unlike the photograph, which

155

showed bent and torn stems and leaves, the composition was balanced, the flowers apparently perfect, the petals as though etched. He had seen designs like it before, on linen and wall decorations in exclusive shops, which his mother—and, he expected, Jeanne—could not afford.

He whispered, 'You want me to carry him in?'

She smiled and called over his shoulder to the departing guests, 'Thanks. Glad you could come. Good night.' Then in a lowered voice: 'Please stay a little.'

The others left. Sadie looked back at him. He tried to appear casual. Who cared what they thought? He moved around the room. He would have to carry Jean to his bed, probably; he used that as an excuse to go into the bedroom. The boy had obviously been sleeping on the cot to the left, where the bedding was mussed; a double bed against the right wall was neatly made up. (Why a double bed for one person? Relax—if one has a double bed left over from a broken marriage or whatever, one sleeps in it alone.) There were more watercolors and some oil paintings, as well as a large sketchbook and carrying case in the corner next to the double bed by the dresser. A large closet with sliding doors. One was partially open, revealing a corner full of the boy's stuff—some short coats hanging, and under them a soccer ball, part of a croquet set, and boxes of games—jigsaw puzzles, checkers, war games, Monopoly—that an intelligent preteen could play with a grownup, a peer, or alone.

He came out. The guests were gone. He said, 'Just checking his bed. I'll take him now.'

Jeanne had closed her paint box and put the brushes aside. A flat pan of colored water was still on the table. 'Oh, I can do that. Or he can walk.'

In the Marines, at home with a crippled parent, in the police academy, you learn how to pick up grown people—from foxholes, from the ground or floor, from beds, from underneath wrecked cars. Preteens are relatively light. 'Easier for me,' he said.

'He's a lonely child. I sent him to a private school—couldn't send him to the public school around here—and he doesn't have playmates because he can't bring them here. He's used to me. I better do it.'

'It's all right. I've had experience.' The boy came up smoothly and without a jar, resting relaxed and comfortable against his shoulder. Hutkin had taken almost three steps before he felt the body suddenly stiffen and then explode into a flurry of kicks and blows.

157

Jeanne was at his side, lifting the kicker off before surprise had brought Hutkin to a stop.

'Thank you anyway,' she said. 'I'll take him now. You've been very kind.'

'I'll walk!' He sounded like a petulant infant. He wriggled until he got down, but did not kick or fight his mother—though he did look a little big for her to handle. When his feet settled on the floor, he reached for her hand; once he got that, his eyes closed again. He had not glanced once at Hutkin. He seemed already asleep again as he walked with her, and she made cooing noises.

Hutkin heard from the bedroom the slide of linen, the springs, some colloquy about 'your own little pillow' and—again—didn't he want to go to the bathroom first?

She came out, closed the door gently behind her. Her hair was mussed on one side— probably from when she had gone through the flurry. 'I'm sorry, Ralph. He's just not used to you.'

He repeated, 'It's all right,' and sucked on a scratched knuckle.

She came closer. He could see now that the lines under her eyes were etched deeper than he had suspected from a distance. 'You're not hurt or anything?'

'Okay.'

She rested her head in the hollow of his

shoulder and against his neck. It seemed to fit nicely there. The hair was soft. Then slowly, with little sound, she began to cry. Real tears—he could feel the dampness on his shirt, reaching through to his skin. She said finally, 'Such a child. But I think he understood.'

It took Hutkin a moment before he realized she was not talking about her son. And certainly not about him.

CHAPTER TWELVE

They—or rather Birge—had split up the work, and as usual, Charley Hagen reflected, he had got the ditch-digging: going from door to door of the apartments and ringing bells that weren't answered or were answered by people who didn't seem to know what they, and he, were talking about. There was really no limit to such work; somebody could always have been watching from the darkened buildings across the street, or even have noticed movement from glass front windows or sounds through the thin ceilings of the stores downstairs. ('Yeah, I know those joints are supposed to be closed at that hour,' he had repeatedly told what seemed to be successive waves of inexperienced young cops, 'but you never know when a bum or a punk kid climbed in to get out of the cold or to lift something, or a nightwatchman or a relative or even a cop has a key and might be sleeping it off.' Nor, for that matter, when an owner or an employee was late 'taking inventory,' usually starting with the body of a girl or boyfriend. These were always long shots, but he had seen several cases in which that single extra lead was enough to enable it all to fall together.)

Birge had thought that, after those first interviews, the key parties—Brodovic and De Plaissy—should probably not be confronted again until he and Hagan could do it together fortified with new information; so here was Hagen arguing with a maintenance man (saw nothing, heard nothing, wasn't there, works for the owner, not the tenants), then going to apartment 17 to threaten not too subtly that bastard of an English instructor with exposure if he didn't tell everything he saw or heard that night (finally none of it turned out to be of much value), and then to two doors that remained closed despite repeated rings, and despite the fact that he was sure he had heard whispers behind one.

Hagen broke for a late hot-dog stand-up lunch and in the afternoon called in. He got Rodigault, who said that that new kid

(Rodigault was mad that the assignment had been given to, of all people, a probationary) had left a report, and why didn't they teach those punks how to type and spell words like 'male Caucasian'?

'God damn it, read it!'

'All right, all right! Wow! Ulcer time!' Hagen listened carefully until he had picked up the information he thought important, then hung up without saying anything further or waiting until the reading finished. But the 'ulcer time' remark, reinforced by some things the department physician had told him at the last annual checkup, did have its effect. He came out of the booth, took several deep breaths, swallowed half a Rolaid, and walked with steady if not slow steps back to the stairway. He did not start to trot until he was opposite the rock poster.

At apartment 27 he rang the bell—two long ones, leaning on the button heavily, as though that would somehow make it louder. When that did not bring an immediate answer he rapped sharply on the door, making the wood rattle in the frame, and called out, 'Police lieutenant! I want to talk to you!' He was not going to tolerate any more ghostly whisperings behind doors that stayed closed. At the same time he observed the other closed doors from the corner of his eye. Anybody that showed curiosity would be visited later.

Whispers. Then a soft throat clearing. He pounded again. 'All right, all right!' a furry male voice said—as Rodigault had said a few minutes earlier—'Christ!'

The door opened partway and that guy they called Harold (in the phone booth he had glanced at the names that Shepak had given him: Harold Feldhaber) stuck his head out—long hair in all directions. Hagen pushed the door slowly, but strongly, wider, so that Harold had to step back.

'Well, what *is* it!' Harold said. He had on the same blue jeans as on the night of the murder, but his chest and feet were bare. He shivered, his arms across his chest. None of these guys seemed to be much when it came to muscles.

'I want to talk to you,' Hagen said and stepped inside. A few feet ahead of him some kind of gypsy or peasant skirt disappeared quickly through a flimsy curtain held up on a sagging and shaking string. That was one of the girls; where was the other? Maybe working—somebody had to. 'Just routine. We're checking everybody on this floor.' He pretended to consult his notebook while he sized up the place. Apparently they had tried to create some kind of dumb entrance 'foyer' by that curtain. It was dark; there were cushions and wadded clothes on the floor, and a clinging, if vague, odor of old pot smoke.

Hagen closed his book. 'Of course, you were awake when it happened and came outside. That makes you special.'

'Jeez!'

'Let's go inside.' He pushed through the curtain. A larger, brighter but no cleaner room: mattresses, more clothes, scattered books, a table, parts of a stereo connected by wires and needing a dusting. To the left a door to some kind of side room was closing. There were two chairs at the table and one against the wall. 'All right. Sit down. You better put on a shirt if you're cold. There are enough around.'

One chair had a blue flannel shirt thrown over its back; the man put it on. He sat on the chair and curled his toes around the legs. He did not look nearly as cocky as he had the night of the murder. He said, 'Why so early?'

'It's afternoon. I have to go by the clock. You work nights?'

'Well, I told that cop—policeman—all I knew when he talked to me outside. You know. That morning.'

'That was just the preliminary investigation.' Hagen sat down, opened his notebook. 'We want more information.'

'Well, I told all I knew.'

'We'll go over it again anyhow. You always forget something.' He tapped his police department ballpoint on the scarred table surface. 'Besides, I don't think you told us everything.'

'Well—' Harold was apparently undecided whether to be indignant or cool—whether to project the most satisfying image or to avoid trouble. The best solution for a guy like him, probably, Hagen thought, would be to try to con the police and then brag about it, but his head seemed to be too woozy. He ran spread fingers through his hair and tried to pull the strands down. 'Who told you that? Why would I hold anything back?'

'Don't you know some things—some facts—you haven't talked about yet?'

'No. I don't remember any.' He brought his hands down and his face hardened with suspicion. 'You been talking to a girl named Millie? Well that flake—'

Hagen bit his lip. He had been so eager to follow the lead that he had almost given the kid away. Like a recruit. He said, 'No. We just got the idea from the way you been acting. You like to spread the bullshit around some, don't you? How much you know?' He brought his hand down on the table sharply, mostly to distract the other. 'All right, let's get down to the facts. You were up at the time

Wesley Gowen was killed. Right?'

'I don't know when he was killed. Nobody told me when. I'm not going to say I was when I don't know.' Deep breath. 'An' you can't make me.'

'You hadn't gone to bed yet that night and you told Corporal Shepak that you had been in this apartment since midnight and you came out later when you heard the police officers, and Gowen was already dead. So were you up here when he was killed or not?'

'Well I guess so...'

'You said you were having a high-class discussion with your girlfriends about Buddha and the Eightfold Path.' He glanced at his notes to get it right. The little bastard was not going to upstage him. 'Wesley Gowen was murdered down that hall.' He jabbed a hard forefinger toward the door and then swung it toward the right, in the direction the body had actually lain. 'He was murdered brutally by being knocked on the head and there must have been some hollering and then he hit the floor and he was hit again.' Hagen paused and glared at Harold, holding his glance steady till he thought he saw the other start to shrivel. Actually, he knew that this apartment was some distance from that first stairway and on a slightly different level—not like 17, where that English teacher was—but it seemed quite

165

possible that Harold had heard something, and that was what he had been hinting about in Hutkin's report. And if he were lying or bluffing, let it come out now and let him suffer. 'You were talkin' peaceful subjects—all intellectual, no hollerin'—and you heard or saw something. Or you heard and then went out and saw. It was something like that.'

Harold was starting to sweat. That was a good sign. 'I never said I knew or was sure about anything.'

'You're a fellow who hints a lot. You hint about what you know, and sometimes about what you don't know. But *I* know you heard something. I know because I checked to see how far sounds like that would carry from there to here when there isn't much noise, and I *know*.' It was a reasonable supposition anyway.

'Even if you hear something, how can you be sure what it is? It could be anything. Lots of noises around here.'

'Think of everything you heard—human voices—that might have sounded unusual. Try maybe, say, between one and two o'clock.'

'Well I did hear—once—a kind of . . . I guess you could call it a cry. A holler.'

'Like what?'

'Oh—mad. Angry, I guess. Kind of wild,

excited.' Harold was watching Hagen with some visible anxiety. Probably, right now, his chief concern was to get off the hook. And that was useful.

'High? Low? What?'

'Not real low. Man gets excited—could have been a man got excited, raised his voice, sort of thin. Maybe something like a scream.'

'What did it say?'

'Just a holler, no words I could hear.'

'Not low. Then it could have been a woman too?'

'Maybe.'

'Or a man? Either one?'

'I guess so.'

Hagen thought he saw that door to the side room open about a half-inch. Or maybe it had been open all the time. Should he go, drag out the girl—would she be the Sadie that Hutkin had described?—and see what she had heard? But probably, now at least, she would not go beyond what the boss-man had said. He closed his notebook and said sarcastically, 'You been a big help.'

Harold Feldhaber allowed himself the ghost of a smile. Maybe he thought he had won after all.

★   ★   ★

As Hagen came out the doorway he was sure he heard something that sounded like a thud or thump. Maybe something flashed along the wall, but he couldn't be certain because it was below the steps on the lower level and the lights, as always, were low. He saw no one there, but a couple was coming up the second stairway, close to him, and he looked toward them as the source of the sound.

But then he decided that it couldn't be them. They were a young couple carrying grocery bags, their heads close together in earnest low discussion; the woman had a purse in her free hand, and the man was rummaging in his pocket, apparently for keys. He looked up, saw Hagen, and they moved faster. Hagen thought for a moment that he would stop them, but he was getting tired, and they looked like the kind who worked or went to school all day and slept deeply at night, arms around each other. He had better prospects, and he was curious about that thump and how far that sound had carried.

He came closer to the few broad steps to the lower level. The couple—stepping rapidly while trying not to be too obvious about it, the man holding the key extended in front of him like a wand—opened their door and disappeared behind it. Hagen stayed close to the right wall. In one doorway he thought he saw something strange—a white patch in a roughly hexagonal shape. Maybe more than one. What were they? Papers? Circulars that whoever swept hadn't swept?

Then a boy came out that doorway and kicked the objects, and they turned and bounded across the hall. A soccer ball— alternate brown and white hexagonal sections. The boy kicked it again. He must have been kicking it before, Hagen thought, then ducked into the door when the couple came up, maybe because he wasn't supposed to play in that hall, or whatever. No one played with him. He turned, slowed the ball, and then kicked it the length of the hall in the direction away from Hagen—past that open stairway, past the last apartment doors of Brodovic and De Plaissy—to the far end. The kid must have been pretty good because Hagen could hear the dull smack as the ball struck the plaster, despite the distance.

So the sound would have carried to apartment 27, and possibly beyond. He was right about that, at least. Probably.

CHAPTER THIRTEEN

'You saw this stuff from Washington.' Birge waved the sheets at Hagen.

'I didn't get a chance to read it all,' Hagen said. 'How come we don't have some of that in *our* records? How come we had to wait for fingerprint ID?'

'He changed his name since he came here.'

'Changed it to Brodovic?' Hagen raised both eyebrows.

'Mostly he changed the spelling— Anglicized it—you know, that Polish-Slavic spelling you like so much. Dropped a syllable. Changed some pronunciation, I guess. It used to end in something like w-i-c-z.'

'Between clearing your throat and sneezing.'

Birge sighed. 'Be sure to tell that to Inspector Maravich. Anyway, that's the reason our files don't have it all.' He turned the pages. 'Not that there is very much. Came to this country when he was about ten. Thereabouts—after the Nazis, no birth certificates in that town, in the old country, if they ever had any. Father was a miner till he got hurt. Then he worked as a blacksmith in the SoPac yards.'

170

The eyebrows went up again. 'Horses on the railroad?'

Hagen must have got enough sleep. It was obviously his day to be witty. 'They use blacksmiths to shape tools and parts in places like that.

'Mirko—he never changed that name—had some trouble with local law enforcement. Like most of the other kids. You know—a few sheriff's deputies somewhere, and a couple of big, tough railroad and mining companies whose guards make up most of the visible law. No appeals. He was a kid, he couldn't speak English for a while, fell behind in school, and probably got beat up pretty regularly. New kid, hunkie, and so on.' Birge lifted his eyes. 'I'm just assuming that, of course, but it seems logical enough.'

'Maybe the old man helped out on the beating if Mirko griped about it.' Hagen sucked on his cigarette, his cheeks hollowing. 'The good old days when kids were taught discipline.'

'He got picked up stealing tools from the yard. Where his father worked. Passing them through the fence to some other kids who waited there and sold them. I guess that was one way to be accepted. Obviously they used him. He said later in reform school that he was set up. But probably not. They just used him

171

because he was so eager. They weren't caught and the only evidence was his statement—and that was a lot later, when he was already doing time. During the hearing he kept saying that he was no squealer. The judge didn't understand him at first because of the accent.'

Hagen smiled. Birge frowned and glanced at his watch. 'Well, none of this is very relevant. I know that reformatory. He would be raped almost as soon as he came in. They used to use the trustee system there—the toughest kids to enforce discipline and given special privileges for it, and seldom monitored. But they also went through the motions of having some sort of school there— state law, some of those kids were still mandatory school age. One of the teachers taught art, must have spent a lot of time with him. There was a flap about that teacher, so it's in the record. He told the kids to paint and draw what they saw and felt, and then held an exhibit of their stuff, including Brodovic's, in the state capital and invited critics and a reporter to come see. The reformatory director didn't know what he'd allowed until he heard straight from the governor's office. Teacher got booted—from the school as well as the institution, and I suppose he's still selling insurance.

'But Brodovic got the message strong, and I

don't think he's ever been back home. He had all kinds of jobs while he painted, or studied painting—foundry worker, door-to-door salesman, laborer, post office Christmas help. He was even a club boxer for a little.'

'Think I knew a boxer like that. Tried to save his hands until he met a couple of guys who weren't trying to save theirs.'

'I think he only fought about three fights. No, I don't know how many he won! But he did send some kid to the hospital with a blood clot before he quit.' Birge frowned, and thought a moment. 'Well, that could be interpreted at least two ways. Anyway, probably not important. Came here, the closest big city, where there are museums, art schools, foundations, women's clubs, galleries. And women, some with money. And sometimes customers. He got to be pretty good at being a personality—making appearances and pitches, applications for fellowships. Simple, intense—plain strong man painting the plain truth, like that teacher had taught him.' Birge frowned again. Did he really know enough about this field to make judgments? Or even detailed descriptions? Especially before Hagen, watching him with those narrowed eyes? 'Not enough money, of course. He was working as a short-order cook when, I guess, he got the idea for that restaurant. Kind of a natural—cheap rent and fixtures. He's his own floor show, his own advertisement, provides his own decorations. Has his own gallery and is his own critic—the only one that counts. And, of course, he's got his own claque. Hopeful artists come around, I understand, and paying customers to watch the artists, all to admire. And he gives lessons.' Birge sighed. It was remarkable how much in the painfully gathered reports was tedious and irrelevant. He tapped the sheets. 'Naturally not all of this is from the files or Washington. I called the art critic at the *Star*, and had one of their people read part of the stuff in their morgue.'

'What about that school? A con?'

'It's not licensed. But private lessons don't have to be, and that's what he says he gives, so nobody checks. Who's to argue? There's no law, and he's his own authority on what's good. The students don't complain. Only people with no artistic taste.' He cocked an eyebrow at Hagen, who was staring at the ceiling, as though he hadn't heard.

'Naturally somebody like Gowen would be attracted,' Birge said. 'I'm surprised he didn't come much earlier.'

'Or somebody like our boy Hutkin.'

'Maybe. Maybe not. I mean, to swallow it all. Hutkin's older; he's been around more. I think it's just relaxation to him. Besides, probationary or not, he's a cop.'

'He better be.'

'But Gowen . . .' Birge paused.

'I read part of that journal,' Hagen said. He stretched. 'That girl, De Plaissy, she teaches some in her apartment too.'

'Yes. But if it makes any difference, she's recognized, teaches at the university. If it makes any difference.'

'Only to guys who ain't got no taste. And lousy English.' Hagen reached over and flipped the sheets with his forefinger. 'Brodovic was raised playing rough, where nobody gave a damn, including him. He's used his fists and maybe other things to hurt people, and I didn't hear any regret in those papers. He uses people to get and keep what he wants and to make himself a great man. And pardon me, but I don't get the impression he would be artistic and gentle with anybody he thought might be cutting into the territory. And along comes Bright Eyes. When are we going to go and lean on him?'

'Very soon,' Birge said.

PROGRESS REPORT
RE: GOWEN, W. Hom. file # G4584
TO: Birge, S., Capt., Hom. Div.

FROM: Hutkin, R., Pr. Ptlman (Spec. Assgnmt.)
Pursuant general instructions arrived Petit Montmartre, 3412 Evergreen St. this city 10:02 P.M. 4/25. Object, if possible, to try to enter into confidence Brodovic and De Plaissy, particularly the former, to discover information about actions and attitudes night of murder that might be easier to get in relaxed circumstances. Subjects still consider respondent to be fellow suspect...

Brodovic said, 'You talk to the police today?'

'No,' Hutkin lied.

Maybe because, by his standard, it was early and there weren't many customers around, Brodovic was sitting alone at his corner table. His illumination was electric—the light over the coffee urn reached his table—and the candle was not lit. His pipe was in the ashtray. A tiny coffee cup, apparently one of a series because the waitress had taken two empties away when she had brought this one, was at his elbow. She had turned to watch when Hutkin entered, and then had gone back to the kitchen without changing expression or asking what he wanted. Though there were two other patrons

176

in the place she seemed to be waiting on Brodovic alone.

'Why?' Hutkin asked. 'They been putting pressure on you, Mr. Brodovic?'

The artist looked at him steadily and calmly for a moment. He did not immediately ask Hutkin to sit, nor seem disturbed that he kept him standing. Hutkin had noticed that Brodovic's manners were seldom neutral—as they seemed to be now—and sometimes subject to rapid change. Sometimes they were mellow and effusive—especially to new guests on entry, or when something pleased him; then, when his interest flagged or he was feeling displeased or irritable in the early morning hours, he could be abrupt and dismissive. It was not, it seemed to Hutkin, that he was intentionally boorish or rude; he simply turned away, obviously unwilling to waste more time and attention on what seemed profitless. Hutkin had the impression that he was being briefly weighed in that scale: Was he—and his information—weighty enough to be worth the time? What did he know?

'Please sit down,' the artist said suddenly, and Hutkin concluded that he—or the information that could be gotten from him— was that weighty.

Of course there was always the possibility

177

that Brodovic had an idea what he really was. Or—and this might not be altogether bad— that he was cooperating with the police.

The older man picked up his pipe. He said, 'Ralph? That's your name—Ralph?' Hutkin nodded. Brodovic paused a moment while he lit the pipe. 'Didn't you really know this boy that died?'

'No, I didn't. I understand that he came in pretty often, but I don't remember him. Could have seen him and not noticed, I guess.'

'Well, a quiet kid.' Brodovic had used a kitchen match; he now shook it out. 'Nobody noticed him much. And lately—he sometimes didn't come to the restaurant at all.' His eyes moved toward the door. Hutkin remembered that the last evening classes at the branch university let out at 10:30, and some of the students might be arriving soon. 'A terrible thing,' Brodovic said. 'A terrible thing! And right upstairs.' He seemed suddenly bored with the subject; his voice trailed off. He said, 'Did you come to see Jeanne?'

'Well, I hope to. But not only her.' Hutkin thought: Get him to talk about himself—the cardinal rule. While waiting for the results of his police application, Hutkin had worked briefly in a department store in which new employees received some truncated Dale Carnegie as part of their training, and he

178

remembered that one very well.

In the indirect and reflected light, turned up a little this early, he could see a few paintings along the side walls a bit more clearly. They all seemed to be the same artist, or at least in related styles, though, he noticed, the subjects did vary to some extent. Toward the front there appeared to be a few landscapes, and he saw two figures— apparently portraits. Small lights were clipped to the frames on a few, probably for lectures or private examinations because they were not lit now. The closest and most clearly visible picture had been signed with a flowing signature in red that started with a *B*.

It was a very stark picture. A tall, black, old-fashioned mine tipple was projected harshly against a red sky (was that dawn? sunset?) with cables hanging down like gallows ropes from its huge, turning wheels. A doomed procession of almost obscured gnomelike figures wound up a long road— endlessly, since the road ran off into the frame—to disappear into the base of this monster. Some had their mine lights burning on the front of their hardhats, throwing feeble shafts of light—muddied by fate and apparently badly mixed colors—about a half-inch into the gloom, but bringing no real relief. They did not seem to speak to one

179

another or even cluster occasionally into protective or friendly groups—only marched, bowed, into the maw. The red of the *B* and the wavy line that made up the signature seemed to represent dark fires far underground, waiting.

'That's a strong painting,' Hutkin said, staring at it. And innocently, as if he didn't know: 'Did you do it?'

'Yes.' Brodovic's eyes rose and stayed on the painting.

'Very, very strong.' He did not know what other word to use. 'Is that the way it was?'

'I paint the truth. Not photography.'

'Well I mean . . .' Damn it! 'I mean . . . it was painted a long time ago, or at least a few years, wasn't it? About . . . the way things used to be?'

'I paint it when I first came here, set up this place. Maybe a little before. About what I remember. My feelings.' He moved his pipe to his left hand and held up his right toward the painting, turned so that the angle between thumb and forefinger seemed to form part of a frame; he stared through that for a moment. It did not seem to Hutkin that he would be able to distinguish much detail—the picture wasn't strong on clear detail and the light was not good—but Brodovic lowered his hand, satisfied. 'It's the truth. It doesn't change . . .

Well, if I did it again, maybe I wouldn't do everything the same exactly . . .' He smiled.

'That's very interesting. You wouldn't paint that way exactly now?'

'No, no change to the subject! A little to the technique, maybe, some places.' He raised both hands and moved them before the painting as though remodeling portions. 'I paint for over twenty years. I learn all the time. The eye gets better, the hand—quicker. Never change the truth! But—a little more attractive now.'

Despite everything, the picture had some raw power. That would not have been improved by becoming 'more attractive.'

The artist was on his feet. 'But I am not just a one-subject painter! Everything—all life—is a subject! Look here.' He strode down the row of paintings. Hutkin was impressed, again, with the breadth of his shoulders, the way that dark hair fell smoothly, with only one strand of gray, down to the wide collar. Brodovic reached up—a straight thrust like a jab—and yanked a switch on a small picture light. A landscape—a park scene, apparently, and Hutkin suspected it was from the picnic area at Willow Park in the city, though he couldn't be sure—trees, a bandstand, a horizon, flowers, and some varicolored blobs that might have been picnickers. Heavy brushstrokes, flakes that might have come from a palette knife, and depressions from a thumb. The technique didn't seem very different, and he wondered briefly whether a tranquil scene could be successfully portrayed by attack. Well, maybe some guys (that fellow Van Gogh?) could do it. Some guys. 'Very nice,' he said. 'Sort of dreamy.' Brodovic snapped off the light. He had made his point.

But Hutkin's eyes had started to wander to the next picture before the light went out, and he stopped short. Brodovic had apparently not hung his pictures in order according to chronology or subject, and this one must have been one of his earliest. That much Hutkin could see from the style. But again—if he could say 'again'—that too obvious symbolization, an even greater amateurishness ... and the power. It was actually more a cartoon than a painting. In the center and dominating everything was a huge, black wooden chair, very solid and square: high back, clamps on the arms, a round piece just above like a metal skullcap with wires, attached to the top of the back and hanging over ... waiting. A harsh light, its source off the picture to the left, glared down on and towards the chair, projecting a shadow or a series of shadows that, from the distortion caused by the angle and the corner of the

182

room, became a slanted cross—or perhaps the heaviest of repeated crosses, each smaller and fainter than the one before till fadeout. And toward the left, against the wall, cast by the same light, another shadow close to the floor—a man being dragged . . .

'What's that one?' Hutkin asked.

Brodovic turned to look and gazed at it a moment. 'I was a kid then,' he said. 'Lots of promise, but I didn't know much.' He returned to his table.

At the door a young man wearing sneakers and a cardigan, a small party on the sidewalk behind him, put his head tentatively inside and looked around, but Brodovic did not rise to greet him. Something else was bothering him. The waitress went toward the front just as the young man started to withdraw the head.

'It is a very interesting picture,' Hutkin said. It sounded like an echo. 'You're—uh—trying to say something, aren't you?'

'Say something, *say* something! What does that mean? What am I, a salesman? "Brodovic *used* to say something when he was young!" Wonderful!'

He seemed to explode. He raised his right hand—rather, his fist—in the air. Those powerful shoulders heaved. The chess players—once more present at their nearby table—looked up for the first time in Hutkin's experience. Those who had started to enter paused and turned toward the voices. But Brodovic paid no attention. 'Saying something! An artist works, polishing his craft—'

'But I didn't mean—' Hutkin tried to interject. For a moment he wasn't sure that the bigger man might not strike him. But he thought—and hoped—that the shouting had not been directed solely at him.

'All right! Saying something. What does that one say—' He swung his arm around, looking for somebody else's painting, or at least one that might illustrate his point, but there weren't any. 'All right! What do they mean, art should say something? A telegram? What does this—what does Picasso—say, hah? Each time a different painting. Girls with their eyes on sideways—what do they say?' The arm now made a strong gesture of dismissal, thrusting forward almost as though pushing someone out. 'Damn fools, writing for the papers! Damn fools, coming in here!'

Some of the damn fools who had come in there looked up again, to see if he was glaring at them. They did not answer, but there was some whispering. As though she had seen it all before—it was part of the show, the atmosphere—the waitress calmly readied the

184

table and showed the guests to it. They followed. Her eyes seemed a little larger than usual, though, to Hutkin.

It had to be an old argument. Brodovic must have gone through it before—maybe not so publicly, but probably in the same place, since he would need the pictures to point to. 'Does beauty *say* something? Always dumb stories for children and papers to understand?' Perhaps in time the new guests would cease to be embarrassed, accept it, talk about it volubly on the way home. Along with the paintings, the tablecloths, the candles, the whole thing.

Not that it was necessarily a deliberate performance. Brodovic wanted to speak, to answer old criticisms: He spoke. He was a natural, plain man! He had endured a lot, and he answered back. He sat down at the table. The voice, the hand, rose again, but this time more calmly, though with no less certitude. 'I speak with painting. All my life! Landscapes. Portraits. Religious. Everything. I was not born rich, nobody gave me; I worked, I suffered.' He looked up at the painting of the mine, àlmost directly above his head, once more. 'Plenty. When I was young, very hard. *Very* hard.'

He gestured down the row of paintings to the end. There were two far portraits—

Hutkin assumed they were portraits—but they weren't clear. Two people—one had a red background, the other a green. Maybe they were impressionistic or something; maybe it was just lack of proper light. He was not even sure of the sexes.

Hutkin said, 'Did that boy who was killed—Wesley Gowen—did he say anything about these pictures? Did you show him?'

'He liked that one.' He raised his hand toward the mine tipple, although this time he did not look toward it.

'Yeah? What did he say?'

'He said something about the poor people. I don't know.' Brodovic was losing interest. 'They aren't just poor people. They're miners. You have to know that if you want to paint. Things like that. The truth.'

'He liked it though. I do too. He was sympathetic with them.'

'Sympathetic,' Brodovic said. The word was flat. Something else had caught his interest. More heads appeared above the cabaret curtain, apparently discussing whether to go in, and he was watching them.

Hutkin hesitated about what to ask next. Could Gowen have done something to rouse that fury that Hutkin thought he had partially glimpsed? Had Gowen reached for something this man had particularly prized—and what

186

did he prize? But how could Hutkin ask any of these questions—particularly since he had done such a lousy job of leading up to them?

'Well, it's interesting that he liked that one. I wish I'd known him better. What ones didn't he like? Did he criticize any to you?'

'Who cared?' Brodovic stood up, his eyes still on the window. 'I wouldn't tell the police, but I tell you something. I didn't like him. He was a punk kid. I wish to God he never came here. I had to tell him once to take his whore and get out!'

Hutkin gaped. He said, 'His *whore*? Who? What happened?'

That touch of violence returned. Brodovic waved the right hand as he had before; his voice rose too, but not enough to carry clearly over the drone of conversation in the room. 'He came in here, in *my* place, with this little bitch! This chippy right off the streets! I had to tell him—he heard me and she heard me but I kept it down for everybody else—I said, "Get her out of here and don't do that again if you want to come back. You learn respect for the decent women here." A chippy right off the streets! Poor people!'

His left hand kept squeezing the hot bowl of his pipe as though unconscious of the pain. He stared down at Hutkin for what seemed a long moment.

187

Then the front door opened again, and the sound distracted him. He put the pipe back in the ashtray and briefly rubbed his fingers. He said, 'If you want to see Jeanne for a little, her class should be finished.' A couple had come in and he went to meet them.

CHAPTER FOURTEEN

The Journal of W̶e̶s̶l̶e̶y̶ W. A. Gowen
Mood
 'And I have come upon this place
 By lost ways . . .
 And by what way shall I go back?'
 That pretty well expresses the way I feel. It's by MacLeish I think. (Check.)
  . . . like coming into a friendly cave—a cave of the arts, maybe. Away from that cold platform, the stink of the big trucks lumbering backwards to get their sacks and packages, the men hollering words like 'fuck' at each other, whether they're cursing or kidding, even whether the girls are there behind the counter or not. And most of the other conversation everywhere about what hurts, or what can get me money. Or sports. Or whether those girls will, or did, put out, and to who. (whom?)
  Into the warm dark place, dark paintings all

188

around. And close the door. Smell of thick, strong coffee, funny kind of haunting music— some Hungarian, some Greek I think but I'm not sure. A world where other things count. Maybe not really, but close enough.

I know it's another restaurant, and the owner expects you to buy. He sends the waitress over, and the prices aren't cheap, and he watches to make sure that I order, and more than once. But what is reality, outside of the pictures and understanding in your mind, and your feelings? (I won't say 'heart.' I think that is the kind of sentimentality I should avoid. Maybe there's a better word. Check.)

Even the owner—I don't think he's only interested in money. He's the artist who painted all the pictures in the place. At least that's what I'm told. The people I talked to—some students from the university night school, and some people who come there all the time—tell me that there aren't any other pictures from anybody else—not even a calendar. The candles flicker against them and you can't see clear—just occasional glimpses—but right now I like it better that way, they're part of what I feel. Pictures on the walls of a museum are something else. People standing outside, looking, maybe deciding what to think.

A girl says that there are some very pretty pictures, watercolors—flowers in a vase

189

against a white background, two birds circling, a ballet dancer, that kind of stuff—in the ladies' room, and she heard they were painted by the artist's wife or girlfriend (he's named Brodovic [sp.?]). But the man says that's not art. She says it is, and he says it's considered design or decoration or illustration. I noticed a picture different from those in the restaurant in the men's room—a football player in the air, catching a pass over his shoulder—every fold, every muscle clear—but I thought it was probably from a poster. It's a small, dark—and smelly—room anyway.

I might add that many of those who come to Petit Montmartre are students, and I used to be careful what I said, because I only had a few night school courses myself. But night school seems to be mostly for people who want to study things like computers or accounting or things like that, and when I asked about literature, most hadn't read as much as I had. I stay away from subjects like philosophy. And I don't talk about art. Or feelings. But I listen.

Observations
'I have heard the mermaids singing, each to each.
I do not think that they will sing to me.' (Eliot)
I've got to keep up on my reading. I wish I could sometimes—not always—discuss it with

190

someone. I had thought I might be able to find someone like that at the restaurant, but it hasn't really worked out. Unless you get the same assignment in class somewhere, others don't usually know what you're talking about, or they're not really interested, or they think you're trying to show off. And they argue, for no reason I can see. There's a girl who comes around maybe as often as I do, named Millie—I don't know her last name. She's thin, nervous, and I can't help it, but the way she wears her hair reminds me of the Statue of Liberty. She's bright, and I think she's kind, but every time you say something she thinks it might be an attack. How did she get that way? From the others? And they?

Are they basically different from the fellows at work—except maybe bigger in mouths and education and smaller in fists? Some, I'm sure, must be different.

Time! I don't have enough time! Sweat for an hour and I have maybe two sentences! . . . Ma works so hard. I promised her I would paint the wood trim.

Oh God I hate that overtime! I try to read in bed and the page is a blank and I pass out. And I drag around. We need the money.

That truck exhaust. The guys make jokes about it—'Stay out here long enough and you'll sing soprano!' 'You'll puke lung soup!' Like it really is a joke.

People

I talked to the owner—Brodovic, if I have it spelled right—last night, and it was interesting. The way to talk to an artist is about his painting; you don't have to go through as many fences. I didn't start out to talk to him. I went over to about where he usually sits, but he was off somewhere. I wanted to get a look at the paintings closer, in better light, and I got stuck at the first. I didn't hear him come up until he said, 'You like them, eh? That one?'

I said I did—I had to be polite. But I wasn't sure. Maybe I hated it. In those shadows the light wasn't much and it wasn't clear. For a minute, when I stepped aside and my own shadow moved off, it looked like a nightmare—or one of those horror pictures on Saturday TV—or worse because you know it's not acting—twisted black dwarfs marching steady into that mountain. If that's what it was.

He started to talk about how he painted it; he held up his hands like he was outlining or blocking out parts to show what they are and how they fit together. But that's not the way I saw it. The painting itself is actually kind of muddy. I thought it was that way on purpose— the real technique—because that fit the feeling.

192

He kept talking. I don't know if I could have interrupted, but anyway I didn't. He has one of those deep, full voices, and that kind of accent, and sometimes he would wave those big hands and that voice would soar. He was young, he says, when he painted that one; he wouldn't paint it, or that way now, but he likes to keep it in that position because it attracts attention, and then people go on to look at the other paintings and see how he developed. He talked about technique. I said yes, it was very interesting.

But was that why I really stopped? Do we know why we do things? Is that why and how he painted that? . . . I wish I could find answers, if possible from one book and maybe one teacher in the time I got.

. . . Millie said last night that she had dug out and listened to Sgt. Pepper again. She also mentioned 'Eleanor Rigby' and 'All the lonely people.' The Beatles, she said, are still relevant; and she didn't care, but she thought the critic who said Sgt. Pepper was as important as 'The Wasteland' was probably right. I said nothing and listened. Her friend Mr. Hurwitz—he has this mild, calming voice—said, after all, they were both written a good while back in other times, and also can you really compare apples and oranges? I just

193

listened. I better read them again . . .

*. . . I had seen the woman they called
Brodovic's wife a couple of times before—she
would walk through and smile at people and
the last time she said 'Hello' to me and
smiled—but this time she came and sat down at
the table I was at. Maybe Millie sent her or
told her something I said. I don't know.
Anyway, she sat down and smiled, and said,
'I've seen you here before. I understand you
liked some of my work.'*

*It's not easy for me to talk to people directly
and closely the first time we meet; it's especially
hard with a woman like her. She has these
large, very dark eyes and hair; a kind of broad,
white forehead—sort of Spanish, but not quite.
And that sort of quiet calm. She is about 30,
maybe, or a little less. I told myself that it is
part of her job or function, as the owner's wife,
to be pleasant; it doesn't have to mean
anything.*

*I asked her if that picture of the football
player (I didn't want to mention the men's
room) was her work.*

*'Yes. I did that for an advertisement,
originally. Then I worked it over again.'*

*I said I liked it. For an advertisement, in
fact—I had trouble coming up with the right
words—I thought it was beautiful, so much*

194

more than it had to be.

She laughed. She has these perfect teeth, and I couldn't see a filling. 'Well, that was a wonderful thing to say!' Yes, she too thought it better than it had to be; that was why she had worked on it again. She put her hand down on my forearm—I had changed my shirt, but I still wore my work pants (many students just wear jeans) and I suddenly felt very shabby. She said, 'Thank you. That was a very nice compliment.' She said, if I was interested, she would like to show me more of her work . . . No, not here. She laughed again. 'My work down here is in the washrooms, and you've already seen the only one I'll let you in to.'

She had to leave soon. She had to finish an assignment upstairs. But she would see me again. Was I an artist? Or wanted to be one? I said no. Then later, when she was about to get up—the waitress had come and whispered to her—I said well, not that kind of artist; I wanted to be a writer . . . She smiled and then left.

That's the first time I actually told that to anybody. Of course Ma knows. And I told John. But I was just a kid then, a kid confiding in his brother.

. . . Ma again talking about how she wants to get in touch with John. (She calls him John

195

Wesley. It's a good thing she never named me Wesley John.) She says, 'I want to tell him that we are getting by, with your salary and my disability and a little bit here and there, we are keeping the home up. It's a nice home, and Wesley is taking good care of it, and come visit us as soon as you can. I know you are very busy out there in the West, but when you can...'

He never wrote us—we don't know his address! He was gone for years in the army and as soon as he was back he just took off, no goodbye, leaving me stuck! I don't want to see him again. I said, Sure, Ma, just as soon as we can...

...when most of the group was gone, and the rest as usual were arguing and not paying attention to anyone except themselves, I noticed that Jeanne still had that half-smile like she was listening, as she kept working. I thought I would try something. I said, 'Jeanne, you know that last tornado that almost hit the city? I think the next will hit this building.' I didn't raise my voice, kept it ordinary. 'I think it will hit right here and kill us all.'

She kept up the smile, and she nodded. Maybe she murmured something, I don't know. She was on an especially hard part, and I watched her brush, how it moved in her hand. After another minute when she must have noticed that I wasn't saying anything else she kind of glanced up, smiled again, and went back to her work.

So she doesn't really listen. Not always. She works very hard and keeps at it, and doesn't want to hurt anybody's feelings, and they don't notice because they are always full of what they want to say. I wonder how long this game has been going on. And nobody else noticed. Maybe they don't really care; they have somebody who looks like a listener. I think they would talk to a telephone pole.

I said very softly, 'I love you.'

I guess she heard the sound of a voice again, so she got that little smile, and made that little nod, and kept on painting.

...I waited outside her classroom, figuring that was probably the last class and then maybe I could talk to her. I didn't know exactly where she was teaching, and as you might expect, nobody I asked knew either, but I finally found it because I knew the art classes were in that remodeled warehouse the school took over when it expanded. I looked through the panels in four doors before I saw her.

I can always tell a classroom, at least in night school. There's the dust that you can't see but that never quite settles and you can smell, and somewhere there's the sound of somebody's

197

hard heels, and there's always kind of an emptiness, even when people are there—especially at night. Gyms are the worst, but halls are that way too, and some classrooms.

How was I going to explain why I was there—especially in front of all her students, some of whom might be as crazy as me? I had no business there from her point of view, even in these circumstances, 'being neither father nor lover' (who wrote that?). But I had to see her once more at least, and I couldn't in the restaurant. And she had always understood, or acted like she wanted to. Though it was never anything like this before.

Then the classes were over, and the footsteps and people talking, and scraping desks. They came out and some talked and others walked by, but nobody paid attention to me and I was glad of that. Hers was one of the smaller classes, with easels, and I could see her inside, still talking with a couple who wanted extra attention—there are always a few like that and I was wondering if they would let go, and if I would just have to hang around on the outside. You always get nervous and imagine many things in a situation like that.

She came to the door and saw me, and smiled a little—not as though she expected me, but as though me being there wasn't too far out, and she finished her sentence and then said to

198

the fellow pestering her—something I guess like well, try doing it that way a few times and let me know next week and pardon me—and she came over. A strand of hair was hanging down—I think she must have put her hand, or a pencil, into her hair—and she was tired. But she smiled; she always smiles.

'Well, Wesley! A nice surprise! Are you taking classes here now?'

'No. Not now. I just wanted to see you for a minute. If you can spare the time.'

'Of course. An even nicer surprise. There's a coffee machine downstairs, and some tables we can sit at . . . It won't take too long, will it? I don't like to leave Jean alone.'

'Not long. I just wanted to tell you that I won't be coming to the restaurant anymore.'

'Oh? I'm sorry. Are you leaving town?'

'No, nothing like that.' And I started to tell her what Mr. Brodovic had done.

She quit smiling; her lips got thin. She said, 'Let's go down to that coffee machine.'

We got the coffee, though I don't like it much, and she chose a table behind a pillar—though most of the others looked like computer and accounting people rather than her art students. I told her the way Brodovic had talked to me and Rosajoy.

'So he talks about whores, does he?'

'Well, you understand, it's not that she is

really anybody close, anymore.' I kept talking like that. 'I won't be seeing her much except maybe to try to help.' I thought she wouldn't believe that, but she wasn't looking at me and she seemed to be thinking of something else. 'But he shouldn't have insulted her. And I don't see how I can go back now.'

'I have something to say about that. You're my guest and you can come back any time!' She got quiet then again, staring hard over my shoulder like she was daring someone. I shook my head but I don't think she saw it. 'All right. I can see why you wouldn't want to. So you're welcome to come straight to my apartment, without bothering about him at all. You know what days.'

Then she smiled, and it was like the other times. 'You can start tonight if you want. I missed my ride. Would you drive me home?'

...she has those dark lines under her eyes. When does she sleep? She teaches, takes those free-lance assignments, takes care of her son— I'm sure she'd like to do fine arts on her own, but never gets the chance. She pays for the boy's private school and gets up—or is still up—to get him ready and see him off, and is there when he gets back ...

She's always pleasant. But she's caught. (Like me?) ...

And what of that boy? I know he talks—I've heard him through the door, when I guess only his mother was there, going a mile a minute— but as soon as I—or we—come in or even knock, the clam closes.

He sits there quiet, big-eyed, in that chair in the corner or under her worktable. He listens; when she asks him to do something like carry drinks, he does it—no argument, no confusion. She is proud of it, I don't know if he is. When does he *sleep? I guess those times when he just gets up and goes into the other room and shuts the door. She usually goes in after for a few minutes and we hear whispering, and she comes out and says don't worry, our talking won't bother him.*

She says he doesn't have any friends close— that school she sends him to, which she knew in her girlhood, is far away—and there are no kids for him to play with around here. There are, but probably the same kind that rip off packages from our trucks at work when the guard takes a break. Twice on my days off when I came in the afternoon I heard him hitting or kicking a ball in the hall as I came up—his private croquet and soccer field, forward and goalie for both sides; he stopped as soon as he heard me, and waited for me to go. He is very polite in his way, stands quietly to a side. *I said hello both times, and he didn't answer . . . Ma says I was very quiet when we first moved to the new house and I knew nobody, and then when Pa died, she says, I didn't speak hardly at all for almost a year. A pale wandering ghost, she says. But I don't remember it. She thinks because of my sickness, but that was later . . .*

He's the one Jeanne really loves . . .

. . . I went to see Brodovic. Mr. Hurwitz said it was none of my business, and they wouldn't have told me if they knew I was going to do something stupid like that, but I thought I ought at least to talk to him. All right, he's not the father, but he has some responsibility, they lived together for a while, he must have some time and money, why can't he be decent? Naturally I chose the wrong time. I knocked and waited and knocked and waited and was going to leave when he hollered who is it? and then couldn't understand me when I hollered back. He finally yanked the door open and stood there and glared at me. He was wearing a torn, fuzzy bathrobe put on crooked, and his hair wasn't combed. He has a small bald spot; I never noticed it before. When he finally recognized me, he sort of pulled me in, like he didn't want to holler at me in the hall, and closed the door.

'What do you want?'

'I want to talk to you. If I may.'

'I have no time to talk. Fast. What do you want?'

I guess he just got out of bed or something. The bed—that big bed that Millie talks about, because she says she was told he keeps condoms under the corner brass knob—was jammed against the wall and wasn't made. There were pictures and some wine bottles against the wall and some junk on the floor, but his easel isn't here—that's in the studio, by the street windows, and a curtain cuts it off.

'I want to talk about whether you don't feel you can do something—'

'I don't know what you're talking about. Did you want to sign up for lessons?'

'No. Not now, anyway. I think you should be willing to face up—'

'I have no time to talk now.' He had his hand under one of my arms and practically lifted me off the ground with it, and had the door open with the other. 'I will see you later. Goodbye.'

And I was out in the hall and the door closed. He hadn't thrown me out, but it was almost the same thing.

I think now that there was a woman behind that curtain, and they might have been in bed together when I knocked. Maybe the

203

Hurwitzes are right. Still, nothing's really changed. Something must be done.

That poem fragment:
'By words, by voices, a lost way—...
    And by what way shall I go back?'
It is MacLeish.

...I know some of the worst now. My God, the way people have to suffer! And always the best people!

CHAPTER FIFTEEN

'We're going to see the woman first,' Birge said. 'De Plaissy.' He thought he had better explain that before Charley started to give him a hard time about why they weren't putting the arm on Brodovic, but before he had a chance to continue, the big Buick hit a pothole; since the shocks were gone, everything rattled, including their teeth. The department procurement division insisted on keeping these big ancient buses on the street because they had figured out by computer that since the city got gasoline wholesale, the same way these cars drank it, it was still cheaper to keep them going than to buy the newer, more efficient cars. Maybe they thought it also lent their higher-ranking detectives prestige to be seen in the kinds of limos that movie gangsters used on the late show.

'Try missing a hole,' Birge said to Connelly, the driver. 'See how that works out.' The city's streets matched its cars.

'Shake, rattle, and roll,' Hagen said. 'All right. Why her first?'

'You got all that background information. Hers is the most complete. You did a good job.' Compliments sometimes soothed the savage detective.

'Judy did the most important part. She's great at pumping nice old ladies that wouldn't let me in the door. So? We also got background on Brodovic, as you know very well. And he's uglier. So why not him?'

Birge sighed. What Hagen said about Judy was, of course, very true; she was almost invaluable. But he had a pretty good idea what she would make of the way he said it.

Hagen continued: 'What about De Plaissy? You consider *her* a major suspect?'

Birge shifted tactics and emphasis. 'Okay, we got a few minutes. Let's give Brod another going over—could he, would he, did he?' He kept his voice casual. What he did not need was Hagen's invariable response to the hint that he was being patronized or lectured.

205

'Drill, drill,' Hagen said. 'So we can throw out "did he" in the sense of objective evidence right away—no eye-witnesses, no smoking gun with fingerprints, no reported threats or evidence of planning. And he and the waitress both swear that he was in the restaurant at the time, whenever that was. Not necessarily to be accepted at face value, of course.'

'Very good indeed!' Birge said. He wanted a cigar. The doctor had said no, so he pinched the old one in his pocket. The transmission seemed to be making an unusual number of strange noises and that made him even more nervous. 'Could he? We've already chewed this over. In terms of physical strength, temperament, history of violence, and probably ruthlessness if he wanted to get or keep something bad enough—yes. Right?'

'I don't know. I keep reading that it's always that little mousy guy next door who cries at movies.'

'Physically in terms of proximity to the scene? Not sure, but probably not. Now ... *would* he? Which brings up motive. What could Gowen have, or threaten, that could bring on homicide?' He sat quietly for a moment, staring at a yellowing pit in the window next to him and the way it distorted passing headlights. 'Well—I better not get too far out. Brod is a former fighter with a bad temper who already sent a professional boxer to the hospital. Wesley Gowen had a weakened bone. A homicide doesn't have to be murder. As Haskell says, it could be bad luck. Even a mistake.'

'What happened to the hammer theory?'

'A professional's hook, bare-knuckled, to the exact spot? Possibly enough; I don't know. We'll have to check. And a hammer does imply probable planning, while a fight does not. Not as likely, anyway.' Another pause. 'In any case we ought to have another go at motive. Why, under any circumstances, would he want to hit Gowen that hard, even if he didn't think it would be crippling or fatal? The only thing I can think of is De Plaissy. And I think we agreed that between Brod and her that had been dead for some time.'

'Well, his vanity isn't dead. How would you . . . I mean, *I* wouldn't like to be replaced by that kid.'

'You know he hasn't tried lately to interfere with her boyfriends. In fact he's encouraged some. You read Hutkin. And . . . well, it goes further than that.'

'Oh, these tough assignments! I want one.' From the tone Birge knew that, as usual, Hagen was becoming impatient with his detailed analyses. He knew the argument: How many homicides in reality rather than in a textbook or a mystery could be explained entirely by logic? And what of all those that made no sense at all? Practical argument by a practical man ... and the lame Birge answer was that you still had to have some frame of reason or order to check out first. In case sense did apply. Somehow.

'Well, I was trying to make a point ... From your expert-alley point of view, wouldn't Brod be likely—and with some fury—to punch out anybody smaller who attacked him or even, as he saw it, gave him a very hard time?'

Hagen turned his head slowly and stared a moment at Birge. 'So the mouse strikes again, eh? Good God, why would that kid want to take on Brod?'

'You read that journal. I guess you did. He wouldn't actually have to start a fight, or intend to. And he wouldn't be doing it for himself. I don't think that kid would ever be doing anything like that for himself.'

Hagen's eyes stayed on his superior. Birge knew that look and what went on behind it—including, probably, the grudging admission that the old man's arthritis hadn't yet got to his brain. 'You mean you think she put him up to it?'

'She wouldn't have to. Maybe not even want to, consciously. But she hasn't told many people, if any, her story. She stayed away from her family when she needed their help and now she won't talk to them. Who else would she tell, of those she saw around? And how many other people are there like Gowen? She wouldn't be human if she wouldn't, finally, want to tell somebody.'

'That kid?'

'Think about it. Who else, in detail? After he first learned the gossip part from others, of course.'

'And you think he would try to do something bright like appeal to Brod's better nature head-on?'

'You read the journal. He seems to have tried, even before she told him.'

'Wouldn't she ... *know* what might happen?'

The car bucketed along. They hit a short stretch of cobbles and abandoned streetcar tracks that had not yet been asphalted over, and Birge watched the yellowing window rattle in its frame. 'There's always that possibility.'

They were silent. They were getting close, running parallel to the river. Hagen said, 'Not much of a case, is it?'

'A matter of taste. Preference in kinds of homicide.'

'Speaking professionally, of course.' The

streets had been crowded with late rush-hour traffic when they started, but, in this neighborhood, before the theater crowds started to come, there were relatively few cars. In the drizzle some were putting on their headlights. 'This is an appointment?'

'She's expecting us. It's still early, for these people, and she's not teaching tonight. She'll be alone.'

'Except for her kid.'

'Well I hope—I expect—she'll send him somewhere.'

Hagen had been there more recently than Birge, and he had, with Judy's help, compiled the report on her background and situation— so he would know that there was hardly any 'somewhere' else the boy might go. But Birge said nothing more, and thought that if that knowledge made Hagen feel superior for the moment, it was still inadequate compensation for all the overtime without pay he was putting in.

'And one more thing,' Birge finally added. 'A painter tends to get paint on his knuckles.'

*   *   *

But in a sense they were not early enough. Hutkin was already in the restaurant. As they passed the front, going toward the door to the stairway, Hagen nudged Birge and pointed above the cabaret curtain and the picture frames toward the probationary. Birge had already seen him—flannel shirt, lank sandy hair falling over his forehead, cigarette and beer bottle being handled as though they were props. 'Cop' wasn't written on him, but neither was 'bohemian.'

But worse than that—what was he doing there so early? His reports always started close to midnight. 'This ain't the FBI,' Hagen said in a hoarse whisper—by which he meant that the department did not try to control twenty-four hours of an officer's day—'but this ain't bright.' It was not. Hutkin could come up to see De Plaissy and find them there. There would have to be better coordination. And—Birge winced slightly, remembering how Hagen had recently used the word—more professionalism. 'Boy doing a man's job,' Hagen said.

'All right,' Birge said, his voice as low as Hagen's. Hutkin had not yet noticed them in the little strip of window above the curtain, nor, apparently, had anybody else. Birge pointed toward the stairway and they went ahead.

They met no one on the stairs. (Were any of those posters on the wall her work? Probably not—with her expenses, including the boy, she would have to concentrate on money, the ad agencies. And she would take better care of her work than these peeling specimens.) In the hall, someone was entering 17. He looked back, saw them, and closed the door quickly.

At the De Plaissy door Birge raised his fist to knock—then held back. A voice was singing—a woman's voice, rising and falling gently and deliberately, but clearly—a simple song that reminded him of something dim and remote in his past—probably a roundelay, probably in French. Then on the refrain another voice came in, reedy, a little breathless, but seeming to gain confidence as it rode alongside the woman's soft, sure tones. They finished the refrain; the woman laughed, and applauded twice. Birge knocked, bringing dissonance: the world intruding.

Whispering inside. Mostly the woman's voice; Birge recognized three words—'I told you'—in her murmurs. Hagen started to knock harder and Birge waved him off. She said, 'Come in, door's open,' and Birge turned the knob and stepped inside.

The woman was behind her worktable—as Hutkin had more or less described her: painter's blouse, reading glasses hanging from a thin chain around her neck, a grease pencil stuck into her hair to rest above her right ear.

She smiled slightly and nodded. She had obviously been working while she sang, and she had laughed. The boy was standing, close to her, in front of his chair, a TV table with a half-empty glass of milk and part of a peanut butter sandwich next to him. He seemed frail, but that, the father in Birge recognized, was at least partly because he had reached that late prepuberty stage in which the leg and arm bones suddenly shoot out, leaving the flesh stretched out from pink and gray knobby elbows and knees. The milk glass was quivering; he had apparently just put it down. He held a wooden ball in his right hand that he must have just picked up. He did not look friendly.

'Hello,' Birge said. He nodded to both, the boy first.

The child turned toward his mother. She nodded too, giving him a larger smile than the detectives had gotten. 'Go ahead, Jean. We've already discussed this.' He motioned toward a door leading to another room. He had sung while they had listened outside, but he did not speak now. 'No, darling. I think it would be better in the hall. Go on. I really do. There shouldn't be many people there this early... You promised.'

The boy went into the other room, took some equipment, stood in the doorway and regarded them a moment, then finally went out. Birge held off speaking until Jean had gone. He found himself almost fascinated by the way those grasshopper knees turned and bent—like badly articulated stilts, he thought, like Roy's about thirteen years ago—and yet were somehow efficient. The effect was exaggerated by the shorts, which the boy had outgrown. He nearly said, almost aloud, I hope she gives him long pants for school.

There were surprisingly few chairs in the room; if she held classes here she must keep the seats in another room—or the students stood at easels. There was a low, sagging, small sofa and cushions on the floor against the walls. Hagen sat on one, his arms around his knees—no doubt, the older man thought, illustrating how slim and limber he was. Birge moved the chair the boy had used a little farther from but facing the woman, and sat on that. He went through the ritual of taking out his pad and arranging it on his knee.

She took the pencil out of her hair and smoothed the strand back. She took a final look at the drawing on her table and turned to face them. Her chair was higher than theirs— the schoolteacher in her class, at a psychological advantage—though a less attractive woman might have worried about the appearance of her knees and hips from that angle. She said, 'Well, gentlemen, I guess you feel you didn't cover everything when you last interviewed me.' She was polite and perhaps 'cooperative,' but that was all.

Birge said, 'We're just going on with the investigation. We have some new information.'

'Oh? What? May I know?'

'Mostly general. Background stuff.' He moved the pad on his knee a couple of centimeters while he thought about which way to go. He usually knew before he started interviews what points he wanted to cover or discover, but the paths to reach them often had to wait till he saw what he was facing.

'You knew, of course, that Wesley Gowen was very fond of you?'

It was remarkable how cold that face could become. 'You said that before, as I remember. And I told you then that was a very bad way to describe our friendship. Our close friendship.'

He sighed. Probably a wrong start; even so, he couldn't just leave it there. 'Ms. De Plaissy—are you aware that Mr. Gowen kept a journal?'

She was pale before; when the pallor increased, the hollowing of the cheeks and the shadows under the eyes seemed suddenly to stand out. 'No. What . . . is that exactly? A diary?'

'Partly. But he wanted to be a writer, so it wasn't just a list of what happened but descriptions, observations, his feelings. So on. Some was just practice, I guess.' He waited.

'Well ... I don't know police procedures. And methods. But ... do you really have a right to do that? Isn't that personal?'

Hagen snorted. Birge said quietly, 'I wish—very much—I had had a chance to read it *before* his death. And, I think, so would you.'

He turned over the top sheet of his pad—which contained nothing but doodles—to the first clean leaf. Time to switch tactics a little. 'He expresses considerable anger at Mr. Brodovic. Did you know that?'

'Why?'

'Why was he angry or why am I asking whether you knew?'

'Why angry?'

'Several reasons. The first important one was the rough way Brodovic talked to him and to a girl he had brought to the restaurant.'

Birge paused. For a while they had been hearing the boy playing his one-man game in the hall, and Birge wondered if the landlord knew about it. The sounds were sharp; obviously he was not using the soccer ball Hagen had mentioned but that wooden ball he had taken out—when it hit something the crack carried. Now it hit their door—it must

216

have been aimed directly for it—and the wood rattled in the jamb. The woman looked toward the door but did not say anything or call to the boy. When the reverberations had died down, she said, 'Yes, I know about that. Yes, he told me about it, and he said that he couldn't come to the restaurant anymore after it. I agreed with him—and I told him that he could still come upstairs directly to see me. The whole thing is typical Mirko—selfish, insensitive, and boorish.'

'Well'—Birge's tone was curious rather than probing—'but what if the girl was really and obviously what Brodovic called her? I think many restaurant owners draw that line.'

'In front of both of them—and all the others—openly like that? She's a human being too. Women are. Or don't you think so?' She had recovered most of her color. Those large eyes, very cool, rested on Birge. 'Obviously you don't know Mr. Brodovic very well. Or don't appreciate him. And, pardon me, but I also get the strong impression you don't understand Wesley, though you have been reading his private papers.'

Birge sighed. He noted that his hand, holding the ballpoint, was not entirely steady. For the first time in a long while somebody— this woman—was getting to him. 'Did *any*body understand him? We all tend to see what we want to, and I didn't even meet him. That's not my job anyway. My job is to find out who killed him. And maybe why.' He put the pad away, tired of manipulating it. 'As I interpret that journal, Gowen's dislike of Brodovic grew although he only saw or talked to him a few times. In fact the man almost became an obsession with him—he saw him as ... oh, a kind of malevolent force that threatened people. The kind of thing he had always hated. At least that's what I got out of that journal.' He paused. 'And I don't think he could have reached that conclusion entirely by himself.'

From the corner of his eye he could see that Hagen had shifted his attention from the woman to him, and to the extent it could be done from under lowered lids was staring at him. De Plaissy straightened up on her work stool, and her feet slid from the footrest until the toes touched the floor. Birge went on: 'From your experience, how would Brodovic react to a direct challenge—an insulting one— a demand that he show more consideration? More responsibility? That he come up with more support money?'

She was slow to answer, as though not certain at first that she had been asked a question. 'He wouldn't be very patient. I said that.'

'Would he use his fists? Especially if his attacker were a man smaller than himself?'

'I . . . doubt that he would. These days.'

'He could? He has in the past?'

'Yes.'

Possibly he should give her some rest now. Hagen, if asked—or in charge of the questioning—would insist on pressing on (though Hagen in charge of the questioning would not have handled it this way from the beginning). Birge could not entirely agree . . . but he was tired, and the feeling kept growing that he might not have much time . . .

Her voice was flat: 'What support money are you talking about?'

He did not answer directly. 'Did you know that Gowen did confront him that way? Went to his apartment—apparently when he had someone else there—and made those demands?'

The color drained again. 'No, I didn't. God! When?'

'I don't know exactly. Gowen didn't date all his entries. But it was recently.'

'That was in the journal?'

'Yes. With other things.'

'Did Mirko hit him? Is that why you're asking?'

'No, he didn't quite hit him. He was rude and dismissive. I'm not sure he understood what Gowen wanted. Maybe that made the difference.' He inhaled a slow deep breath and took the pad out again. 'There's the chance that later Gowen bucked him like that once more—maybe stronger—and this time Brodovic did understand. And that one never got into the journal.'

He waited. She finally said, 'You're saying that Mirko may have killed him in a fight. Or a beating . . . Isn't that what you're saying?'

'Exploring the possibilities. What might have happened and what might have led up to it.' Now, if he was on the right track—and really short of time—he would have to close in. He turned the leaves back to the doodles on top, put on his reading glasses, and looked down at them as though they were notes. He kept his voice as calm as that of a pollster. 'Ms. De Plaissy—when did *you* first meet Brodovic?'

She did not answer. He peered at her over the glasses—and then back at the pad. 'I don't have the exact month and year, but you were seventeen. I think not long seventeen. You can correct that if I'm wrong.' Again the glance upward, the waiting, the silence. 'You were pregnant. You didn't want to go home. You didn't want your family's help—or, probably, their criticism . . . You haven't revealed who the father is.'

'I'm glad you left me that much.' Her voice was tight, as though it had barely squeezed its way through her windpipe.

'It's relevant to us only in that Brodovic is not the father. You told us that yourself. We're just trying to determine background circumstances that might have helped bring on a fight. We're not just prying.'

'I can see that. How did you find this out? I didn't make Wesley's mistake of putting my private history and feelings on paper and leaving them around in the hope they would be respected by people like you.'

'We investigated, as we had to. Now let's go on with it, please.' Another deep breath. 'The story we have is that when you were out of places to go—or that you were willing to go— you came here.' That story was from the social services records of the city maternity hospital where she had given birth. She had told the social worker—either in a weak moment or somehow to meet requirements for assistance—that she had gone into the restaurant, newly opened, unnamed, to get out of the cold and because she didn't know what else to do. Birge had a vision of her— younger and more childlike, but perhaps even prettier—sitting crying at a table as the place emptied, and a younger and handsomer—and maybe also a softer—Brodovic coming over to find out what the matter was. But he couldn't be sure because only they would know—and for that matter she might not have told the social worker the entire truth—so he had to stick to what could be directly deduced from the record. 'You started then to live with him. But you didn't get along, and he didn't pay for the confinement; you told the hospital you wouldn't go back. You didn't give the name or address. Or any correct name or address. You said you came from Salt Lake City . . . Still, finally you did go back.' He paused again. 'I'll guess. You were weak and had to recover and take care of a new baby—with problems because it was premature—and again no place else to go. And during the years—'

He was going to add that perhaps some kind of apparent father was better than none, and she was willing to do that—anything—for the child. Then he had intended to try to get back into material he was more certain of, had more information about—the financial needs, including illnesses and school expenses, that had kept her bound to her business arrangements with Brodovic in spite of her feelings and her growing professional success. But she didn't let him finish because she began to scream. It was a strange kind of scream and it brought their heads up sharply, not sure at first what it was—starting deep in

222

her throat and rising, rising without a break. In a short moment it was joined by a pounding and kicking on the door and a wild rattling of the knob, since the spring latch had automatically clicked into place when the boy went out.

Whatever Birge had been feeling, his way toward trying had obviously failed. He said, 'All right, we're very sorry you feel this way. We won't bother you further now.' He could have added, as he had done occasionally after an unsatisfactory interview, that they would probably be back later. But he did not.

*   *   *

Hutkin had come early with the vague hope he might see her before the others—before, he told himself, he was even officially on the clock ... And didn't he have the right to use his free time as he pleased as long as it didn't hurt his work? In fact he could probably prove that it would *help* the work: more exposure at the scene, free overtime, and even the expenses of drinks out of his own pocket ... Eventually, drinking his Schlitz and relaxing, it seemed to him that the faint twinges of guilt were gradually warming to dim glows of virtue.

He knew she had no classes that evening,

either at the university or her apartment, and that was another reason for coming early. She would be more likely to stop in the restaurant; then he could say hello and wasn't this a pleasant surprise? He also knew that the regulars came in much later. That was a relief—he might get to see her alone.

But she did not come, and after a while he felt more and more foolish, sitting alone and pretending to be casual and contented in an almost empty restaurant—one that seemed particularly dusty and strange while daylight lighted the upper window. When he had entered, in fact, Ginnie the waitress had not yet reported for work, and the boss, Brod himself, plunked down the beer and with an abrupt and businesslike hand took the money... Fortunately, Hutkin thought, I don't have to be embarrassed around that guy; he's always involved in some vital personal hassle that ignores everybody else ... Periodically Brod would stalk into the kitchen to issue orders and anathemas, loud enough for everyone to hear; then he would come out and stare alternately at the door and at Hutkin's beer glass. When Ginnie came he turned over his tray to her and went to sit at his private table, where a well-dressed, middle-aged woman had been patiently waiting, and restarted some old discussion about art, making emphatic points by right jabs toward various paintings around the room.

Well, Hutkin thought, I'll give myself another half hour. Maybe three-quarters...

This early the restaurant was not the sealed-in world it became when the window was black and the candles and jukebox were on— and those who were homebound from work got there. He had watched heads and hats moving anonymously and usually swiftly by above the cabaret curtain—and then the fading light made them shadows. The light and the activity all around the restaurant emphasized something he had hardly been aware of close to midnight—that the walls and ceiling were thin and carried vibrations and noises. He heard feet frequently going up the adjoining stairway—almost always up at this hour—including two especially heavy pairs, in step, like soldiers on the march. Not long after, he heard the boy, Jean, playing in the hall—the sound carried because he must have been using the hard ball and the smashes against the baseboard were sharp and loud.

Hutkin sipped his beer and was debating whether to invest again in a *czardas* on the jukebox to enliven things when he noticed that the sound of the ball had stopped and suddenly had been replaced by a pounding and rattling—not as clear, since lower in pitch, but vibrating part of the ceiling. Perhaps there was a cry. Then these noises ceased. Brod seemed to notice nothing and Ginnie's expression was noncommittal as usual, but Probationary Patrolman Hutkin had his head up, listening. Those heavy footsteps came down, less in rhythm this time; the door opened and immediately after, Hutkin saw two figures he thought he knew move swiftly past. He went to the door, looked, and listened. An old car started, but it could have been any car.

He felt nervous. Earlier Harold had looked in and, when he saw that none of his usual antagonists were there, had immediately left, but Hutkin had been able to ask him about Jeanne and been told that the day of the week, with no classes, she usually devoted to her son and her work. Hutkin had heard the son in the hall, so some change in the pattern might have taken place, and then there had been that rattling and pounding.

Brod got his payment in advance, so Hutkin swallowed the rest of his beer, briefly visited the men's room, and went out without notice, except perhaps from the silent Ginnie.

He started up the stairs slowly, mindful how easily he had earlier been able to hear footsteps, but about halfway he began to trot.

As his head rose above the floor he could see that Jeanne's door was not completely closed. He heard soft sounds, like weeping.

He went quickly to the door (but not, even now, directly—he found himself stepping around the slightly bleached spot on the floor where the body had lain). He hesitated and listened, then pushed the door gently a couple of inches more so that he could see. She was on her stool, her arm across the boy's shoulder, her other hand holding a handkerchief to her face. She wept a little, but the crying sound was mostly in her words to the boy, comforting him: 'Don't worry darling, I'll be all right soon, don't worry, not so bad ... see?' The boy was still, his face close to hers, his skinny legs tense.

Hutkin stepped inside and pushed the door soundlessly behind him, but the latch clicked as it shut and the boy turned. Jeanne looked up too. Hutkin said, 'Can I help?'

The boy stared at him. Jeanne, after a moment, slowly shook her head.

'Am I intruding? Should I leave?'

She shook her head again, but with her free hand she motioned to him to go sit and wait on the cushions by the wall.

He sat there, first with arms around knees, then leaning against the wall. He was glad he had gone to the men's room instead of racing directly upstairs. She talked for a while to Jean, wiped her eyes, finally began to smile. The boy's long legs, as stiff as poles, began to relax. They sang a song together—for the first time Hutkin heard the child's voice, though it was hesitant because he was there. She reminded the child that he was tired, that he had been standing a long time, and so got him to sit in his familiar spot by her calf, under the table—watching Hutkin. She smiled and shrugged at Hutkin and said she was sorry, then went back to the singing and the soft patter. It took quite a while and Hutkin's own legs were stiff when the child's eyes finally closed.

Even then, when she reached down to take him, the eyes sprang open and the boy stared around. But Hutkin had enough sense to sit still this time, and in another moment the boy began to nod, and let his mother lead him to his cot.

She came out and leaned against the door. Her shoulders sagged. She said, 'I'm glad you came.' Then paused. 'I'm very sorry. It's been a very bad day.'

He said, 'How can I help? Please tell me,' and came softly to her.

CHAPTER SIXTEEN

'Sam, I've never known you to be this inconsiderate before!'

He had come home early for the first time in a week—that is, almost as early as he was *supposed* to get off—hoping that he would get some peace and time to gather his thoughts, and this is what he got.

True, Edna had made this appointment to visit neighbors some time ago. True, she was alone a lot in the evenings as well as the days, and she had not really expected him—though she had the dinner almost ready, just in case. Her friends knew he was a busy man and so she could often accept invitations for both and they would understand when she said he had been delayed; it was all right to come alone. But this time he *had* come home—and should she lie and go by herself? Had he wanted to be alone too?

So he had gone, tired and still rumpled, though he had changed his shirt, to sit and make small talk with people he hardly knew, whose concerns seemed mostly confined to the prices at the supermarket, the taxes on the husband's appliance business, and the way teenagers dressed—while he frequently tried to catch Edna's eye to determine when they could leave.

From a general discussion of teenagers their conversation got down to a specific. The neighbors' son had just graduated high school—he was now working at a fast-food restaurant, and people liked him very much because he was so bright and hardworking—but it was too bad such a boy did not have better opportunities. His grades had been mostly Bs with only a few Cs—he had been on the high school paper and even in the drama club—he was not, like so many these days, a drug taker or one who spent too much time with rock music. They had suggested he go to the branch of the state university or at least the county community college, but he was a serious young man and wanted to start his career now—he had a girlfriend, a very nice girl, Edna Birge knew her, she was in the choir . . .

Birge was slow tonight—tired maybe—and it took him a while, punctured by his grunts, evasions, and glances at Edna, before he realized fully what they were getting at. They knew of course that he was somebody with rank in the police department, a captain—Edna would have been sure to tell them that, though he had warned her often enough not to say what he actually did. ('But Sam, they'll read about it in the papers.' 'Let them!') In a moment these people would be hinting that if he would just to drop a word in the right quarters . . .

He was irritated and knew that, the way he felt, he could easily become vocally outraged at being used this way—by Edna as well as the others. He said abruptly, 'He can get an application form in the personnel department. Tell him to use the 14th St. entrance. But I'd advise him to go to college. It may take a long time to work through, and college always helps.' It might take forever to work through—because of budget cuts they were hiring practically no new officers, and cutting staff through attrition, waiting for people like himself to quit, retire, or die. He sat still while Edna explained to them what Sam *really* meant, then he stood up. 'I'm very sorry, but I'm—this is a very busy week, and I'll have to be up early. It's been very nice.' He could not explain—who, including Edna, could understand?—but how could he act as though he believed in any kind of fairness if he treated De Plaissy as he had and then was polite and understanding to these pests?

'Well, it wouldn't have hurt you to listen! After all, neighbors *do* do one another favors.'

He turned and looked at her. 'Are you telling me I should use influence—if I had any when it comes to hiring, which I don't—to give some boy I don't even know preference over applicants who may have waited longer and be better qualified?'

'Oh, you always come in with these official ... phrases. I mean it wouldn't have hurt to sympathize and give advice without breaking any regulations.'

'I did. I told him to go to college. That's the best advice I could give.' He had brought that limo home; he opened the door for her ... Well, finally, he really ought to give her some salve. If he could call it that ... 'Edna, they're cutting the force. They'll take applications but never call, and I can't change that. I didn't want to disappoint anybody. Or get them mad at me for misleading them, damn it! Let him go to college!'

Maybe she accepted it, at least partially, because she was thoughtful as they drove home. (Damn, he thought, there *is* something wrong with that transmission!) She sighed after a while. 'Well, it does seem a shame, a boy who did so well in high school, that he might have trouble outside.'

Even now, it seemed, his mind could not escape Wesley Gowen. He said, 'High school—*and* college—aren't the whole world!' They might even be among the great deceivers. 'I expect he's found that out by now
232

if he's as intelligent as they say!'

She said, 'My!' and pursed her lips, and did not speak for the rest of the short trip.

★   ★   ★

So, since they weren't speaking much anyway, he finished reading his mail and some reports, took a slow bath, said goodnight, and went to bed early. And since under the circumstances he couldn't sleep well, he was up about dawn, taking his clothes out of the bedroom and dressing as quietly as he could in the chilly hallway in the double hope that he might be able to get away before she wakened, and get to the office early enough to do some reading and thinking before the uproar. It's even possible, he thought, that without much traffic I might be able to get that heap to the garage before it breaks down.

But his eggs hadn't come to a boil before she appeared in the kitchen doorway in that housecoat—a gift from his occasionally strange sister Florence—that made her look like a walking tent. 'You went to bed later than I did,' he said. 'I was hoping you might get some rest.'

'Not so much later. Besides, what else do I have to do? Roy's gone. You're busy.'

He sighed. Their daughter had died almost

twenty years ago, but that was in her mind now. And in his. And probably also his retirement . . .

She took over the eggs and added another one. 'Besides, I want to apologize.'

'You? Well, you certainly beat me to that one. But why should *you* apologize?'

Her lips pursed again, but only briefly. 'Well, there are some things I should always know. That are my duty to remember. When you are *that* irritable and unreasonable then either you are not feeling well or something has gone wrong at work. And I should take that into consideration before judging.'

He stared at her as she put in the toast and adjusted the fire for bacon. Then he sat down at the table and began to laugh. After more than a minute he thought he would be unable to stop . . . Well, Charley always did expect that something like this would happen to him sometime . . .

He looked up at her face swimming above him, that tentative smile under the concerned eyes, pulled her to him, and got hold of himself. He had wanted to put her on his lap, but they were both getting a little too heavy and decorous for that. 'Honey—now I'll apologize,' he wheezed. 'Bringing troubles home—all that.' Laughter welled up again; he wrestled it down. But he was more relaxed.

'Thanks. You're a tonic for sore brains.' And souls—the homicide detective's equivalent of the beat cop's feet. 'A great policeman's wife. Now let's have that breakfast together.'

*   *   *

He was able to beat the traffic and get the limo to the garage and to the attention of a sleepy mechanic, and finally to get to his desk before a thousand details distracted him, but by that time most of the euphoria was gone. The scarred desk, the papers, the homicides, the unsolved problems—these remained, and under a gray morning light they were not more cheerful. Still, he would have more time to think, not faced by crises and eyes that demanded immediate decisions.

He had not read all of the journal—it went on and on—he had not had enough time, and much had nothing to do with the people involved in the case and was not police business. But, worse, he had looked at almost none of the other papers. Except for the nudes.

He put the small thermos of Edna's coffee—this morning he would get to it before Haskell—alongside the folder and began to thumb through the sheets. He had noticed that there were magazine cutouts apart from

235

the nudes: an article about a well-known writer; pictures, in no particular order, of landscapes, crowds, streets. He puzzled briefly over them before deciding that maybe a youth who had not traveled and had little experience might want some models for his descriptions. They too were not police business; he set them aside.

Fragments—descriptions of scenery like something from a travelogue; an essay on sexism in hiring for some night school course; the beginning of a short story: 'John Wesley Gooch stopped at the dusty crossroads. He could see no signs, nor anyone alongside the road who could tell him which was the right way. But set back a little was an old-fashioned general store ...' There were also scattered bits or stanzas of verse, sometimes mixed with other jottings, sometimes alone on full sheets of yellow paper. Gowen obviously did not write all of them, but in his skimming Birge found he could not always tell which were original and which copied—evidence, he thought grimly, of his own lack of taste rather than the quality.

As he went through the pile he found more verse about love, and, as far as he could judge, some of the better—and more sentimental— pieces were among the most recent. At least two or three would certainly have been written after he met De Plaissy:

> *. . . for I have dwelt too long in distant*
> *   lands—*
> *Walked lonely, lonely on the people streets—*
> *And too oft in my dreaming felt your*
> *   hands. . . .*

He turned a few more sheets, then saw one that was not typed, but full of scrawled and scattered pencil notes, sprinkled with exclamation points and with the script often slanting upward—perhaps some written at different times and under different stresses. Birge frowned: What if the boy had gone over the edge altogether? That might shed new light on the case . . .

> *How can I live? What kind of creatures are*
> *they!*
> *Lonnie—and Brodovic? He sent men up to see*
> *her!*
> *Wherever I am—whatever I do—especially*
> *out on that platform—I see that sweet head*
> *and tired eyes over that table. And that*
> *haggard child in the hall . . .*

> *Remember Mom!*

I got to do something! Haven't men died for less?

Birge reread it slowly. Then with sudden urgency he flipped swiftly through the rest of the pages to the bottom. Nothing to get hold of. He shoved the sheets aside and reopened the journal, but he found he could not read much or swiftly now. The other reports, including those from Hutkin and Charley, were in the gray police envelope to his left. He glanced at it, but he did not need to read them again. He sat still for a moment. Then he said softly, 'My God!'

Old men are supposed to have slow reaction times, but he had found Hutkin's number and was dialing within a minute. After four rings he cut off the connection and pressed the button to the extension in the outer office. Again no answer. He was muttering to himself when the dispatcher answered the next pressed button, and he said, 'Never mind that. I want three things. First, have somebody keep calling this number.' He quickly read out Hutkin's number. 'Got that? If he answers, call me by radio—I'll be in a car. Now, as soon as you can get hold of Lt. Hagen—I think he's sleeping, so wake him up—tell him to be waiting at the curb.' He might need the responses and legs of Charley.

238

'That's right, right now! And tell the garage to get a car ready and running. And I don't want that old Buick!'

★   ★   ★

Hagen had once been the police department's handball champ; he took the steps two or more at a time, leaving Birge trotting stoically behind. Birge had just reached the hall level when Hagen burst open De Plaissy's door—which had therefore been unlatched—and was shouting, 'Hutkin! Hutkin! You here, damn it?' That noise—probably also the pounding up the stairs—must have awakened and alerted Brodovic because he opened his door almost as soon as Hagen had turned to it, and they started to shout at each other. But Birge was already past, going toward the last door, the one that led to the inside fire escape—that he had thought was a service door when he first saw it—but which, since the hall was empty, must be where the killer would be hiding, waiting for Hutkin.

He yanked it with both hands, thinking that might break the cheap latch if it were locked. But it was only held, and the yank pulled the smaller figure out, almost on top of him. That was a mistake: It threw Birge partially off balance and freed the arm holding the croquet mallet from the confining wall; the wooden

239

head, with the chipped and worn red paint on its ends, came flying in a wide arc toward the detective's temple. Still, under the circumstances, the aim was clumsy and Birge was able to block it with his forearm and strike it down. But to brace himself and keep from falling he had to grab the other's shoulder and squeeze hard. Jean screamed, went down on those knees, and began to cry. Even after Birge released him he kept crying, head bent, holding that damaged, skinny arm.

Despite his own labored breaths and heartbeats Birge could hear behind him doors slamming and voices; he and Hagen must have made enough noise to waken everybody in the building. Then, above everything, the remembered sound of that woman's scream—rising, rising . . .

CHAPTER SEVENTEEN

There are always loose ends.

'She sits up there, and she hates and hates,' Brodovic said. 'She has been full of hate.'

They were interviewing him again, perhaps to round out the story, or at least include what he had to offer; perhaps also—without tipping him off—to see how he was involved and whether any of it was a crime. And finally, Birge thought, they might be able to satisfy Hagen's desire that they 'lean' on him.

'She doesn't have any reason to, does she, Brodovic? And there've been others too, haven't there?' Hagen said.

'Oh yes, I know hate,' the painter said. He looked up at the picture over his head, then down the row. 'Jealousy. Hate. Yes.' He shrugged and turned back to his pipe, poking into the bowl with a discolored pencil.

'But you don't hate anybody, do you?' Hagen's voice was deceptively mild. Birge watched him.

'No, I don't hate. Who can hurt me?' He brushed the shavings off the table and onto the restaurant floor with a quick sweep of the bottom of his hand. 'I have work. I don't have time.' They watched, as though fascinated, as he got the pipe to sucking again. 'Oh ... but I didn't want this. I tried to stop it!'

'Didn't want what?' Birge demanded before Hagen could. Was this fool about to admit to prior knowledge of—or even complicity with—a homicide?

The other waved the tobacco-stained palm. 'These things have happened to her, and to Jean. I tried to help. Ask her. Ask anybody. Even her own family—well, I was the one took her in, gave her a place to stay. Me,

241

Brodovic, dirt from the mines! Not from the West End, where they spit on me! I used to play with the baby, sometimes. He had no other Papa. Still—still—she hates.' He shook his head. But he had warmed to his subject, and he emphasized his points with the rise and fall of that hand. 'Even when she told me she didn't want nothing to do with me—then even—when I saw the boy was in trouble...'

'What trouble?' Birge asked.

'He didn't want to go to that school! The fancy school that keeps her broke! That isn't long ago, after all the years. I told her, he doesn't need it—you know how *I* was raised, how *I* worked?... He said the boys made fun, he wanted to stay with her. He would sometimes hide when the bus came. I saw it— he tried to hide behind the curtains once in my studio; I heard him cry. I couldn't leave him stay there. So I told her. She said, shut up, you have no rights, leave him alone! I took her in, helped raise him, she says I have no rights!'

'We know how you helped,' Hagen said, again in that mild voice. 'You took her into your bed. Gave her a place to stay, all right. She was seventeen, and had no place else.'

'We lived together, yes. I said that. Like man and wife.'

'And then, when that broke up, you sent

men to her.'

'What?'

The muscles played in Hagen's lean jaw. 'I said you sent men up to see her, to her apartment. Some she didn't know. Don't tell me you didn't know what that means.'

Birge said softly, 'Charley.'

Brodovic looked at Hagen, frowning slightly, as though he were humoring some kind of lunatic. 'I don't know what that means, what you're saying. Some men come in, good customers, people who knew her, saw her in the restaurant when we were together, and they ask politely where is Jeanne and will she come down soon, they want to talk to her. Well, when she's mad and won't come down—she's supposed to be my wife, she's supposed to help out—and I don't know if she'll come down and can't keep making excuses. So what can I say? One or two, I told them where her apartment is. Why not? You think I run a whorehouse? She already has some friends, and students, they come up to visit her.'

'And one or two weren't her friends, never saw her before, but probably asked if you knew a nice girl, and you said—'

'Charley,' Birge said, this time a little sharper.

'Well—' For the first time in this interview

the painter seemed uncertain. 'I am a normal man—you know. When a woman says she will not live with me anymore—I am no good— well, I might argue, but after a while I have to do something else. I don't want fights, I don't want the girls to have trouble. I must paint, I have things to do. But if she could find another boyfriend ... I want her to be happy too ... Should I interfere?'

'A regular lonelyhearts,' Hagen said. He caught Birge's look and sighed. 'All right. We'd like to know about something else. Even though you quit living together, you hate each other—'

'I don't hate. I told you. And, you know, we live in the same building, we have interests, we work together sometimes—'

'Did you help support that boy?'

'Well, I help her find work sometimes, we have students, sometimes the same.'

'Okay, you get along all of a sudden. What I'm asking is about the boy. Did you still keep up contact with him, even after you broke with his mother?'

'Oh sure, he comes in my studio sometimes, looks at the paintings. We talk. I know what it is not to have a good father.'

'Was he in your apartment the night of the killing? Did you talk to him then?'

'Oh no. I was busy downstairs, here in the

restaurant. You saw.'

Birge said, 'I saw him in the window of your apartment about dawn, when I left.' It struck him now that he should have thought it strange then that the boy was up at such an hour. Of course he hadn't been sure it was a boy. But then, later, when he found out from De Plaissy? . . .

'Well I must have just left the door open. When I do—when nobody else is there—I let him come in if he wants to. When I'm not busy. He wanders around.'

'You said you came up during the night or at some time for a clean shirt. Was he in your apartment then?'

'I didn't see him.'

'And did you see the body then?'

'No. I never saw the body till this man'—he pointed to Birge—'showed me.'

'So Gowen probably wasn't dead then. And you left the door open. And the boy went in and out. Or maybe he only went in once, because it was a very good place to hide, and Gowen would have to come past it—'

'Charley,' Birge said, 'I've got to call headquarters, on the car radio. I'll need you. Come on out with me.' Outside, away from the windows, he said, 'You're only supposed to ask one question at a time . . . Charley, what are you trying to do? We know who did

245

it. We disagree often, but you don't often act unprofessional.'

'Sam, he *must* have known something about the killing he isn't telling us. He must have known that kid was there before, and certainly he must have known after, when you saw the kid. With that bloody mallet that hadn't probably been cleaned! Sam, he's an accessory! He must be!'

Birge could see that the agenda for next morning's philosophy session was already being laid out—Collender's crepe soles on his desk, Edna's coffee in hand, and the calm medical examiner voice: 'Sam, aren't *we* accessories?'

'Charley, how could you prove a thing like that? From the probably inadmissable testimony of a sick minor?'

'Captain, how can we let it go?'

Birge was tired. After a while everything seemed to become words. 'Remember—"He had no other papa."'

'Oh Jesus!'

'Well Charley, maybe we're lucky—it's not up to us to make the final decision. We'll collect our information, add our conclusions, leads, and recommendations—you can write that one up if you want to and I'll okay it— and turn the whole business over to the prosecutor's office.' He knew, and so did

Charley, what the prosecutor would do with police 'recommendations' about something as tangential as a possible accessory after the 'guilty party' in such an unpopular case was already established.

'Prosecutor's office—the thousand-mission desk pilots.' Hagen examined his polished toe as it gently kicked the broken stucco of the wall. 'Well then ... I guess we better do the same for De Plaissy. You can't convince me *she* didn't know something.'

'After we take away the son you want to indict the mother?'

Hagen raised his head again and smiled. The department dandy wasn't getting the time to properly take care of his toilet; mild tobacco stains were visible on his teeth. 'You're absolutely right, Sam. *We* don't have the power to decide who's guilty. Let's just turn it all over to the prosecutor.'

CHAPTER EIGHTEEN

Some loose ends are self-inflicted.

The message on his desk said to call the medical examiner, who had called earlier. 'He said something like his call was in answer to your call asking him to call someplace else,

247

and so you should call when you come in.' A typical Haskell Collender message.

'Hello, Sam. Sorry to keep you waiting. Our business is always thriving.'

'Yes.'

'You asked me to make that call for you to the psychiatric ward. That's because of my experience with the death trauma, I guess.'

'It's because there is an MD after your name, and I thought they might open up to you a little more than to the police.'

'Some of their finest patients are policemen.'

'Haskell!'

'All right, Sam, no more jokes. They didn't open up much to me either. They say he's regressing—which I won't explain. He's withdrawing, anyway. Sits turned away from everybody, face down and toward the wall.' Birge remembered that bent head . . . and the expression on that face as the boy had gone to his knees, and out of Birge's range of vision.

'They say anything else? Explanations?'

'You want to hear the Oedipus part? Well, really Sam, they can't know anything or much at this stage, and they got enough sense not to guess. Though not enough sense to let up on that jargon . . . well, maybe that's their way of saying nothing. In six months or a year I guess we can holler at them, but right now it's understandable. He's sick, won't talk, won't respond, won't eat. They don't know about force-feeding yet, they'll think about that later. They're watching his toilet habits and other things to see how out of touch he really is. But—you know—they're understaffed; it's not a glamour trade.'

'Neither are we. We're going to have to make recommendations to the court before any six months.'

'Sam, right now you probably know more about him than they do. Did they consult you?'

'They have—or will have—my reports.' If they look at them, he thought—but did not say aloud. 'And the recommendations will come from a joint conference of *all* involved, and *I'll* make it a point to be there.' That was one of the reforms he had fought for. 'A lot of nuts and bolts—not just law and psychiatry— including things like what will the options, if any, really mean for a kid like that. Institutions and so on.' He sighed. Did everything really become just words? 'I'm telling you this for your edification, since you're an ignoramus.'

'I'm humbly grateful. For the compliment too. Be very useful in working with my stiffs.'

'Oh, you're useful sometimes. For instance, apparently they did open up some to you. Did they say how long?'

'No, they say they can't know this soon. And since you're showing a personal interest you should know that in this kind of business usually the only short-term treatment occurs if you're a cash customer and run out of money—not a public charge, with the state paying—as I understand.' Pause. 'Sam ... what advantage for him *to* recover?'

Birge was silent a moment. 'I don't know. Some, I'm sure. In time, anyway.'

'Sam—how did you *know*?'

He meant figure out who did it. They would all be asking that. He would have to phrase it simply: 'The weapon. He only had one. Once I thought of it there was hardly anyplace else to go ... If I were smart I'd have thought of it sooner.'

'Oh, you're smart all right.' More silence. A serious Haskell seemed to be developing on the other side of the phone. 'Sam, I'm not in the psychiatric grift, nor in yours.' That's a novel admission, Birge thought. 'But some plain ideas ought to apply. Did he know he killed? What it meant? Can he face it? And his mother? And like that.'

'Well, sounds logical.' But Birge had found that to get his work done in his limited time he often had to think in even simpler and more direct terms: If a half-crazed child has nothing but his mother what will he do to anyone he sees as a threat to . . . that relationship? What else could be as important to him? And could the detention psychiatric ward provide any kind of a prosthesis?

He asked, 'What about the mother? She there?'

'Waiting room. Almost from the beginning. They've told her to go home.'

'Did she see him?'

Collender sounded a little abashed. 'I don't think so. I didn't check, but I'm pretty sure not. He didn't ask, and I think they think it may be too soon. Maybe he wouldn't know her; it might be traumatic or something. I suppose later. *They*'re in charge now, not mothers or homicide captains.'

'All right.'

'Well Sam, my patients are calling. You know, they don't give me this kind of trouble. You and I might be in the right business after all. More or less.'

'Yes.'

★　　★　　★

Birge had asked that Judy Tersky be temporarily assigned to him again when finished with whatever she was on—guarding a school crossing, something like that—and finally she had come. She was still in uniform—starting to fit pretty tight across the hips, he noted. She was no longer young. Her husband was a city-hall clerk, and Birge understood that she had decided to apply for the force primarily to pad out the family income, and only after the court had ordered the department to hire more women. She had not in the beginning seemed to show great desire or talent for police work . . . She put in for detective whenever tests were announced, but had not yet been appointed. She probably thought that was due to sexism, and perhaps to some extent it was.

He explained what he wanted. She nodded; he had given her similar jobs before. He added, 'Also, I promised Mrs. Gowen I would talk to an editor about her son's work.' He paused. So little of that work was done. And the only editor he knew well was in charge of crime news; Gowen's mother didn't need more of that kind of publicity. 'Tell her— well, tell her I want to think about it a while. I'll pick a better time . . . Thanks, Judy, that's all.'

He didn't hear her leave, and when he glanced up in a moment she was still there.

'Yes, Judy?'

'Well, sir—' She stopped. He noted that she seldom called him by his title, but usually 'sir.' 'Well, sir—you know I've asked you to put me sometime on—well—*real* detective's work.'

'You don't consider this detective's work? You don't consider it necessary? Or desirable, anyway?'

'Oh I'll do it, sir. I certainly don't intend to disobey orders.'

He motioned her to a seat. He said, 'So?'

'I mean *real* detective's work. Going out on a case, investigating—the kind of thing that might make a difference on my application ... and the way they look at me. You see, you're sending me out to talk to these two mothers. I know it's not easy. But they'll say that's just woman's work!'

'Should I send Lt. Hagen? Can you see him trying to explain things to them?' She sighed. He continued, 'By the way, one of them, Ms. De Plaissy, will almost certainly not be home; she's staying close to her son. So it may be less than you thought.' He paused and took a deep breath: 'Now, by the same token, I have trouble imagining you getting the facts out of a bunch of convicts in a prison stabbing, as Charley could. Judy, I've tried to have you assigned to homicide. I try to maintain a team—each doing what he—okay, or she—does best, in a way that we can all work together. Let's get the damn job done!'

She looked at him quickly; her eyes widened.

He said, 'I'm sorry. I guess I'm pretty tired. I won't insist you take the job. No, and if you refuse I won't put it on the record. I can do it myself—never mind my other work. But I don't think I'll be very welcome.' One final familiar thrust: 'Let's make it simple. There are those women out there who lost their sons. You can talk to them and explain things and give them some comfort better than anybody in this division. They might need help from other agencies that you know as well as anyone, and can explain better. Are you going to do this assignment or not?'

'Well, yes sir. I never said I wouldn't.'

★   ★   ★

A final loose thread—at least the last he was going to take care of. Apart, of course, from finishing pounds of paperwork.

Ralph Hutkin sat before him. He did not look very happy or innocent, in spite of the lank, little-boy strand falling before his eyes. It was partly his fatigue, Birge knew, but he did not feel as charitable as he should have. But he tried. He said, 'Overall, you did a good job. About what I expected, and I'm not sorry I chose you. But there was a serious lapse, and

I should have expected that too.'

He turned to the papers on his desk. 'I won't detail that in my report or the evaluation. I won't ignore it, but I'll say something like, "Despite errors of judgment due to youth and inexperience, as were expected," and then go on to talk about the good things. And there were good things. Your reports were better than I had hoped, for a probationary. We'd have had a tougher time without them.' Hutkin's reports were clearer and more complete, perhaps because he was more intelligent than most, and that could be part of his problem.

'I'll put in for a commendation for you. You won't get it because you are probationary and older men might resent it, but mostly because there was no apparent physical danger involved.' There was, but he didn't want all the details to get to the chief. 'Still, it will look good on your record, and you might get a letter of appreciation from the CD or the chief himself, and that would look even better.' Birge paused. 'You have anything to say?'

'No sir. I . . . will say that I appreciate this very much.'

'Well, I'm not quite finished.' He moved the sheet listing the points to put in the report in front of him. These were not doodles. 'I'm going to recommend further that you not be assigned to investigative work like this again, at least for a while. I will say you need experience, maturation, and so on. You might be happy in something like the traffic division. What about technical work? You're quite intelligent—lab work, fingerprint, computer analysis, and so on? Someplace where you won't be as likely to be influenced very much emotionally.'

Hutkin looked at him, surprised. Birge started to meet his eye, then decided not to. 'There isn't much danger of investigative detective work for a long time anyway, of course. You'll have to put in your years in uniform.' But that too would, much of the time, involve direct contact with people in trouble.

'Look, Hutkin—I won't pass any of this on and I won't get after you for the usual misbehavior or corruption. Policemen will always, sooner or later, have money or women tossed their way and very few duck 100 percent. Especially in some divisions or squads.' He had vice in mind, but didn't say it, though the thought of Hutkin on the vice squad made him pause for perhaps two seconds. 'Corruption isn't your real problem. A policeman—especially at the detective level—has to be able to keep some balance and distance. You get involved.'

He waited for some response. Hutkin gave none.

'You get *too* involved.' He turned back to the paperwork—the piles of it. 'Okay, that's it ... Well ... if you want my personal advice ... if I were you I'd think about another career. Not right away; don't put yourself or your family through any hardship or uncertainty. Later, maybe when you have some savings ... Will you think about it?'

'Yes sir.'

'No hurry.' He really should break off and get more rest, as Hagen was doing; if he talked a little longer he might start to back away from his point. 'It really isn't complicated. In your case it might be just being young. But not all people are temperamentally fit to be policemen.'

'No sir.'

Photoset, printed and bound in Great Britain by
REDWOOD BURN LIMITED, Trowbridge, Wiltshire

E